ENCHANTED REVIVALS

STORIES RETOLD - AN ANTHOLOGY OF TALES OF OLD, TODAY RETOLD

TIANA LEBEAU, PHOENYX LEE, COFFEE QUILLS

INEXHAUSTIBLE MEDIA

CONTENTS

THE PAINTED GATE

On the day Old Raving Rodrick finally died, his children wasted no time looking through their childhood home for the things they wanted, then sold the place as-is, including the remaining furniture and decor. I agreed to continue my housekeeping services for the new owners, Candice and Freddy Dumonte. We added cooking and making sure Candice, an artist, ate and slept whenever Freddy was out of town for weeks at a time, working for the government. It sounds like a demanding job, but they made it easy, and I really did it for the company rather than the money. My husband recently passed away, and my daughter lived across the country. Loneliness and I did not get along.

The only part about the job that I didn't like was having to enter the art studio. Three of the four walls were a gorgeous yellow that looked like gold when the sunset hit them. Black paint, glittering with malice, marred the remaining wall, with bramble-like swirls covering it from floor to ceiling. Something about the design unnerved people. Not Candice. She said she liked it and refused to renovate or paint any part of the "charming" house in the country, far away from the busy city. My skin prickled every time I walked into that room, and I wasn't the only one. On moving day, I watched the movers race to get out of that room, and, later, Freddy started avoiding it, too. He coaxed his wife out as often as he could.

Candice told us all that we couldn't see the mystery behind the flawed wall, or feel its inspiration. I chalked it up to her artistic nature and left it be until things started getting weird about a year after they moved in. By then, they felt comfortable enough with me to talk about Candice's mental health, her migraines, and the reason Freddy worried so much while he was away. I grew to love the time I spent in their home, enjoyed working with them, and found joy in my job, even after Candice started acting out.

One day, when I brought some soup and fresh bread to the dining table, I found her sitting there with dark circles under her glassy eyes and ashen skin. She looked drained, and I pursed my lips and narrowed my gaze at her. "Are you alright? You look like you haven't slept in a couple days." I set the food down. "Freddy will give us both trouble if he thinks I'm not looking out for you."

"Yes, Delilah," she said with a smile. "I've been sleeping fine, ate the breakfast you left out for me, and I even walked around the pond as the sun rose."

I felt relieved. The breakfast container was in the dishwasher, and I wondered if she ate or flushed it. Knowing she took that walk in the place she found so beautiful, no matter what time of year, quieted my fears. I watched her fondly when she spent hours down there, studying the plants to get the details just right for her paintings after they first moved in. Now, those outings either broke her creative slump or signaled a migraine.

A few weeks later, I overheard Candice repeat things Rodrick spewed while he was alive. His children often visited me before their father died, filling me in on his worsening mental state. They told me how he raved about Tilly being inside the house, and, when it became obvious he was a danger to himself and to others, Doctor Andrea Marlan hospitalized him, where he lived until he died, continuing to lament over his missing wife.

"Do you have another migraine coming on?" I asked, taking a seat across from her for another lunch. After a few days of her odd behavior, I had to ask.

"It's possible since I am seeing things out of the corner of my eye while I'm painting."

"I wondered about that with how jumpy you've been lately." I gave her a small smile and picked up my cutlery. We lapsed into silence until we finished eating and I took her dishes, stacking them on mine. "You've been more out of sorts this time."

She frowned when I stood and turned toward the kitchen, giving her space to think. I wanted to get the dishes washed before the soup dried too much, anyway, and the two of us could talk for hours when she was like this. Candice didn't let me get far, stopping me with a question before I could leave the room.

"You knew the man who lived here. His wife, too?"

I looked over my shoulder and watched Candice focus on a scratch on the table, picking at it with her left thumbnail. My voice shook when I answered the question. "I was her maid-of-honor, and she was mine." I paused and sighed. "It might be called matron-of-honor when the lady is married now. Not that we bothered with such formalities."

Candice looked up. "What happened to her?"

My stomach dropped. I felt my lungs stop working. The answer sat on the tip of my tongue until I could take in a slight breath. "Let me get these dishes going first."

Candice followed me into the kitchen, watching me load our bowls and plates onto the lower shelf without making too much noise, then I dropped the cutlery into the tray. The two of us padded into the sitting room with two plush chairs, a couch, a side table with two lamps, and a wall-to-wall bookshelf. I sat on the couch across from her and took a deep breath, letting it out in a slow stream, steadying myself to tell a story.

"Tilly was my best friend growing up. She married Rodrick Laramy—her highschool sweetheart—and the two of them lived a happy and active life with two boys. A third pregnancy surprised the couple when the boys were six and five, but a health complication ended up with Tilly in the hospital. She came home with a warning not to try for another baby." Despite being so long ago, the memory still brought up grief that stuck in my throat. I needed a drink, so I excused myself to grab my metal water bottle on the counter in the kitchen, and continued when I returned. "That brush with death caused Rodrick to change. Tilly said he picked up a new hobby, but she never mentioned what it was beyond how weird she found it. Her whole body would shift with discomfort whenever I pressed for more information. Beyond that, though, she did not appear otherwise concerned. See, he would hyper-focus on his projects like you, always forgetting to eat or sleep. He loved her and their children much like your Freddy loves you, so I didn't fret too much."

My building emotions calmed a bit when Candice gave me a self-deprecating smile. I reached into my pocket, pulling out my handkerchief to fiddle with, my fingers tracing the stitched edging to settle me enough to continue. "One day, when she was supposed to come over for our weekly tea, she never showed. I called and called with no answer. The next morning, a police officer knocked on my door, asking to speak to me about Tilly going missing. Roderick claimed he thought Tilly stayed at my place overnight, but when he heard my messages on the answering machine, he realized something was wrong."

"Weird. Did they ever find her?"

"No, and I always found it strange Rodrick had never called me to ask if Tilly was with me. The officer thought so, too. They said it looked like she left town without reaching out to anyone, which was not like my friend at all. She loved her kids and friends too much to disappear like that."

I quickly changed the subject after that, asking Candice about her upcoming art show. She told me about her exhibit. We talked until she decided she wanted to take a nap. I told her I'd get the cleaning done, prep some food for dinner and tomorrow's breakfast, then head home.

I noticed nothing else unusual for a few more weeks after telling that story, and Candice bounced back, never getting that migraine we all expected. It was after Freddy came home and then left on another business trip that she started complaining about her migraine auras again. Her questions about Tilly started up again, too. I avoided them the best I could and watched as she obsessed over finishing one of the best paintings I'd ever seen from her. Her attention to detail, and how the light reflected off every petal, left me awe-struck. One day, I stood in the doorway, watching her paint, and thought I heard someone whisper my name to my left. I glanced at the glittering black paint on the yellow wall and thought I saw a shadow move behind it. When I looked back at Candice, she was staring at me with a blank expression.

I stumbled back, tripping over something on the floor. The sound brought life to her eyes again, and I let it out with a sigh when she shook her head and looked at me with confusion. "Delilah? What's wrong?"

"I could ask you the same thing, girl. Have you eaten or slept since I last saw you? You look like a ghost." I stepped into the room and helped her off her stool in front of the easel, blaming the second shift of shadows behind the black paint on my discomfort.

"I don't think I've eaten yet," she admitted.

"Lucky for you, I have lasagna for lunch."

I led her to the dining room, and the two of us ate and talked about her Northern Lights painting commissioned by some wealthy woman the Dumontes knew. Candice sounded like herself and even glowed with excitement. Once she returned to her work, I called Freddy and told him about her concerning behavior.

"This isn't like her usual breakdowns," he mused. "I'm going to contact her psychiatrist and book an appointment while I'm home. Better safe than sorry."

Though I agreed Candice's safety and wellness needed a proactive approach, I wondered if this was something more sinister. Not wanting to sound crazy, I kept my opinion to myself.

He booked her an appointment. When they returned, Freddy pulled me aside. "She said to monitor Candice's behavior, and that someone needs to be with her full-time. I just can't get time off at this point in the project. Are you willing to stay here while I'm away until I can take leave? We'll pay you more, of course!"

"Sure! I can bring some stuff over. Are you sure it's her mental health, though?" I shrugged when he gave me an odd look. "Nevermind."

He made a dismissive noise in the back of his throat and the two of us ran over to my house to pick up clothes and toiletries to make my stay more comfortable. I still went home whenever Freddy returned. He handled the cooking and took Candice out on dates or day trips into the city to see his brother and her sister. I saw the bright woman we both knew, but the relief only lasted while Freddy was home.

One day, about a month into the new arrangement, I found Candice seated at the kitchen table with her sketchbook in front of her. Expecting to see a landscape design, I peered over her shoulder, but staggered back at the sight before me.

"Oh gosh, Delilah," Candice gasped and jumped out of her chair. She took my arm and guided me to the chair beside her. "Are you alright?"

"Do you know who that is?" I asked, unable to keep my shock out of my voice.

"What?" Candice looked up, sparing a quick glance at the drawing. "Oh, no, I don't think so. Do you?"

"Yes."

"Who is it?"

"Tilly Laramy."

Candice peered at the sketch with narrowed eyes. Her lips pursed as she added a touch of shading, only adding to the realism of it. "Huh. I must have seen a picture of her in the pile of stuff we cleared out."

I knew better. The two Laramy boys picked through the house with a fine-tooth comb after the doctor institutionalized their father. Every part of their mother they could find left this place with them, some ending up at my house. No, this was something more.

"Are you hungry?" I asked, changing the subject. Before she could answer, I stood up and rushed into the kitchen to fetch the chicken caesar salad and garlic toast I made for lunch. We ate without another mention of Tilly.

The next day, when I brought up some tea to the art studio and asked what she wanted for dinner, I found Candice adding black bramble over her commissioned piece. The gorgeous landscape and dancing lights in the sky appeared trapped under the black paint spreading from corner to corner of the canvas. I gasped, scaring Candice. She spun, and a glob of paint landed on the wall. We both looked at it, and as I tried to slow my heart, she grinned. "That's it!" Her attention shifted toward me. "Is it lunchtime? I'm starved."

We left her studio. I felt pushed out of the room when Candice closed the door behind us. I did not see her enter again for a few days. She spent most of her time with her sketchbook, hiding it from view. This rapid change in behavior resulted in a few extra check-in phone calls to Freddy, especially after she started helping with the dishes and cleaning. That was until I overheard her conversation with her sister. I'm not in the habit of eavesdropping on my employer, but my concern grew every day.

"There is something in the wall."

I froze, pushing my back to the wall just outside the door to the art studio. That was what Rodrick's kids claimed he kept saying before the doctor sent him to the hospital.

"No, Jamie, I don't need an increase in medication. The psychiatrist already assessed me." She paused, listening to her sister, which added weight to her assertion; she talked at a normal pace and waited for others to finish. "Look, I just need someone to listen to me. I know this sounds crazy. Believe me, I've been trying to sort it all out, but Delilah has seen it, too. Remember how I saw her fear and sadness when she saw that portrait I drew? I didn't know it was her friend." After another pause, she sighed. "Yes, she's staying with me, so I'm okay. I know you're worried, but wait until I don't check in before you call Freddy, please. Delilah already calls him at least once a day. Okay. Love you, too. Bye."

I found Candice in her studio the next morning, but not at her easel. Instead, she stood on a stepladder with her pallette in one hand and a thin paintbrush in the other. With careful strokes, she added to the garish design on the yellow wall. I watched in horror as she worked. Concerned, I called her name, and after multiple attempts to catch her attention, I approached and tapped her leg.

She startled, looking down at me with wide eyes, almost toppling off the ladder. She pulled an earbud out of her ear. "Delilah, you scared me!"

"Sorry. I was trying to get your attention. Lunch getting cold downstairs."

"Not yet," she pleaded, sparing a worried glance at the wall. "Once I finish the loop. Promise."

I looked to where she gestured with her paintbrush, noticing two thin lines moving from one half circle to another, connecting them. "Fine, I'll wait, but I'll stop you if you keep going."

"Deal!"

She kept her word, closing the circle in the top left corner of the unusual wall. It felt like the room sighed in relief with Candice. Somehow, it looked and felt brighter.

"Are you well?" I asked cautiously as we walked down the stairs. "You seem a little unsteady?"

Candice laughed and shook her head. "I'm fine. Just tired and hungry, I think. Even though I ate breakfast, I'm starving."

"You're in luck. I made your favorite pizza!"

"You're the best, Delilah!"

This continued for a couple of weeks. Candice would stare at that design, check her sketchbook, and attack the next section of the wall. After the first corner, she used thin strips of green painter's tape to create a grid for her to work in. If I asked her to come for food, she refused until she finished whatever she was working on. If Freddy asked about her obsessiveness returning, I told him she always put down her supplies with a smile once it was to her satisfaction. Until she showed more warning signs, we could only monitor her.

With each modification, the wall became less and less unnerving. The number of blank looks she gave me lessened, too, and she slept better. Her appetite became almost ravenous, and Freddy's relief felt palpable.

He became more affectionate, and their laughter filled the home. I spent more time at home during that period, only entering theirs to clean for a few hours each day. When he left, removing the distraction, Candice quickly slipped into her focused state.

One morning, two weeks before the fortieth anniversary of Tilly's disappearance, I saw what I was watching for. Candice looked panicked, claiming she was running out of time and needed to lock herself in the room. I reminded her of the agreement she made with us about the door staying open. It deflated her each time, but she always let it go. The day she sat up straighter with determination was the one I should have paid more attention to.

When I went to fetch her for lunch, I found she jammed the door. No amount of knocking got her to open the room for me, not even the panicked knocks when I heard her talking to herself inside.

"Don't worry, she can't get it. I took the keys in here with me."

I pulled out my cellphone, dialing Freddy, who promised to call the psychiatrist on his way home. Next, Jamie said would be there as soon as she could arrange child-care. My friends Wally and Andrea Marlan, too, would be over as soon as Wally's shift at the fire station was over.

All I could do was wait.

Between the calls and people arriving, I dragged two chairs, a side-table, and some paper into the hallway outside the room. It made it comfortable for me while recording Candice's utterances.

Jamie was the first to show up. She let herself in and met me upstairs, and I could see the worry line etched into her forehead filtering the rest of the way down her expression. Wringing her hands as she sat, she asked, "Has Candy opened the door yet?"

"No." I leaned over and gave her arm a comforting pat. "Freddy said he and the psychiatrist are on the way. I also called a friend of mine. His wife is a doctor, and they are going to come give us a hand, too."

Those words seemed to settle Jamie. The two of us listened to the noises behind the door, reminding one another that things were okay so long as we could hear Candice. It kept us sane while feeling so on edge.

The two of us jumped when the doorbell rang, and I thrust the papers into Jamie's hands to keep notes while I answered it. She took them without a word and jotted down Candice's frustrated muttering about interruptions.

"I know I need to hurry! They'll stop me, and then all of this will be for naught!"

As much as I wanted to stay and listen, I rushed downstairs, hoping to catch the door before the visitors rang the doorbell again. I flung the door open and held the door open for Wally and Andrea. "Thank you both for coming. Let me take your coats. Can I get you tea or anything?"

Andrea folded her hands in front of her, looking around the landing. "Tea sounds lovely, Delilah. Something decaffeinated if you have it." She gave a pointed look at her husband, who quieted any objections. As we walked into the kitchen, Andrea admired the way "The Dumontes did not change a thing."

"No, they liked the charm."

Andrea made a noise of consideration. I watched her purse her lips and drum her fingers on the counter while I pulled down some more mugs and turned the kettle on. "You mentioned some weirdness. Does Candice have any mental health concerns? A family physician?"

"I know she has a psychiatrist involved, but I know little more than that."

Wally rubbed the back of his neck with his hand, looking uncomfortable with the talk of a stranger's medical history. "I'm going to run upstairs and check the door, if that's alright?"

I nodded. "Her sister Jamie is up there. Be nice."

Wally smirked and perked a brow. "I'm always nice, Del."

"Don't flirt with the poor thing," Andrea said, backing me up. We all chuckled, and he gave us a salute and trundled toward the stairs, tool bag clinking against his hip with every step. Andrea shook her head and turned to me, and the two of us sobered. "Is the psychiatrist aware of today's behavior?"

I nodded and filled Andrea in on what was going on, starting with Candice's habit of forgetting to eat or sleep without reminders, her drawing of Tilly's portrait, and the blank expressions I sometimes saw when I disturbed her while in the art studio. "Freddy called the psychiatrist after he and I talked. I think she's on her way, too."

Andrea paused at the stairs, turning around and almost causing me to upset my tray. "Do you know what day tomorrow is?"

"The fortieth anniversary."

"Yes, and Rodrick started his hospital stay ten years ago." She frowned. "I don't know if this is anything more than a strange coincidence, but everything you've said reminds me of him."

"Me too."

As we climbed the stairs, we could hear Wally talking to Jamie as he dug through his tools. "The old git never said anything nice. I'm not surprised his wife left him." He looked up and saw us approach, blushing. "Sorry."

"No, it's okay," I said, trying to smile as I set the tray down and handed Andrea and Jamie some tea. "I didn't like him either. I don't know what Tilly saw in him, but they loved each other from when they were just kids."

"I remember how he looked at her at their wedding," Andrea added, accepting her tea before introducing herself to Jamie. "Doctor Marlan. A pleasure to meet you."

"Hey, I'm Jamie." She accepted her cup and looked at the three of us. "Was Rodrick ever mean to her?"

"Nah," Wally said. "He got clingy after Tilly lost their daughter. She was sick, if I remember right."

"Rodrick rushed Tilly to the hospital, where she stayed for a week. I visited her every day, praying she would get better for us. She did, but only after a devastating loss for the two of them. It changed him. I remember her telling me he was acting strange, but nothing worrisome. Apparently, he spent a lot of time in this room before she disappeared." I offered Andrea the seat beside Jaime, sinking into it myself after she declined. "I think he did something to her. Forty years is a long time not to hear anything."

We all jumped when something crashed on the other side of the door and Candice let out a noise of frustration. "Stop! I'm almost done." We all held our breath, listening as she talked to herself. "No. No. No. If I open the door to let her in, everyone out there will rush in. They won't let me finish."

We all looked at each other with puzzled and terrified expressions.

"Who is she talking to?" Wally asked.

My answer came while I transcribed what we heard, checking with Jamie for accuracy. "The wall."

Wally went to get his crow bar twenty minutes and three tries at picking the lock later. While he was outside, Freddy arrived and the two of them climbed the stairs together. Freddy hurried over to me, thanking me for taking care of everything until he arrived. Jamie and I filled him in with hushed voices, and all of us watched every emotion play across his ashen face.

"I'm going to try talking to her," he said, giving the door a wary glance. "The psychiatrist said she'll stop by after her last session."

If anyone could get through to Candice, it was the soft-spoken, eternally patient Freddy. His presence worked magic on her.

Andrea pulled me aside, her lips pressed into a thin line. "I'm a doctor, and yet I can't find an explanation that makes sense why she sounds like Rodrick did." Her eyes ticked toward the door. "Only she's fighting to let something go instead of keeping it in there." I saw my friend hesitate. "We always believed his prattling on about magic and seals was a sign of his cognitive decline. I don't know what is going on, but I think the clues point to something... more."

Asking if she meant Tilly sounded ridiculous in my head, even though I wondered about it for months now. After all that, I couldn't help myself. "It's getting harder to believe she isn't talking to her in there."

Before we could say more, Freddy walked away from the door and scrubbed his face with a hand and let it fall to his side. "She's asking for more time."

"For what?" Jamie stood up, her and Wally both joining our little huddle.

"She didn't say." He took a deep breath and let it out with a huff. "I don't want to do anything until her doctor gets here."

"I think that is reasonable." Andrea said and stepped forward to introduce herself. They shook hands, and she offered, "Wally and I will go get some food and bring it back. Will you leave them the tool, darling? Just in case they need it while we're gone."

"Don't tell anyone. It's against protocol." He handed it over to Freddy and left with his wife.

Jamie, Freddy, and I sat in the hallway, looking helpless. After a minute of uncomfortable silence, Freddy asked Jamie, "Do you want to stay, or do you have to get back to the kids?"

"I couldn't convince their father to take them a few days early, but I can swing by again once they go to his place for the weekend." She gave the door a worried glance. "I vote you take the door off hinges after this."

Freddy lifted the fireman's crowbar and shrugged. "This'll destroy the door, I bet. Once she's stable, we'll start swapping out door handles."

Jamie stood and hugged Freddy. Much to my surprise, she hugged me as well. I gave her a squeeze and walked her to the door. "Call when you get home, alright?" She agreed, and I waited until she reached her car before locking up and returning to the second floor. "When will her psych be here?"

"Maybe in an hour." He gave a weak smile when I crossed my arms and lifted my brow. "Oh, I am not afraid to break the door down if we need to, Delilah. If I do it too early, it could just make things worse."

He had a point. The two of us curled into the armchairs and watched the door in silence. Exhaustion crept up on me. I fought hard against it, but sleep claimed me until I woke to Freddy banging his fist against the door, calling for his wife.

"You promised me time!" she cried through the door.

"That was before you started talking crazy. Let. Me. In."

She refused, shouting back that she was running out of time. Freddy growled in frustration and slammed both his hands against the door. "I didn't want to do this, but you're leaving me with no choice." He marched over to his chair and picked up the crowbar. After testing its weight, he gave Candice a last chance warning. "If you don't open the door right now, I'm going to force my way in."

"She's almost free. Please, let me finish the spell."

Freddy and I looked at each other with wide eyes and dropped jaws. He repeated the last part of the sentence under his breath. I shrugged and made a mental note to tell Andre. He turned back toward the door and tried to get the claw of the bar into the crack between the door and its frame, all the while muttering under his breath.

"Are Wally and Andrea going to be long?" he asked, his tone biting. I took it as a hint to stop making him nervous. The guest bedroom I claimed looked out to the front of the house, so I wandered to my room and peered out from behind the thin curtains. A vehicle approached the driveway, though I couldn't tell whether it was the Marlans or Candice's psychiatrist in the dark. My fingers released the curtains when the headlights shone toward the house, obscuring my view. I grabbed my knitted sweater, exited the room, and made my way back to where Freddy was trying to leverage the door open.

"Give me a hand with this?"

I took the remaining length of metal in my hands, and with some grunting and coordinated effort, the wood splintered. When the wood let go, both of us ended up as a tangle of limbs on the floor. I pushed myself up on my elbows. Time slowed down. We watched as Candice reached for a painted door handle, both gasping in amazement when the thing became solid in her hand. She turned it, pulling at it, and the painting came to life. The thing opened toward us, the once malicious black swirls now forming a gate and pulsing under the light. Freddy and I sat stunned, neither of us able to move.

Tilly, dressed in her favorite blue and yellow floral tea dress, stepped into the room and pulled Candice into a hug, thanking her. I felt my cheek grow wet with tears as the world went dark.

The hospital psychiatrist sighed and clicked his pen, placing it on top of a face-down clipboard. "Delilah, you know I can't let you go until I know it didn't result in something serious." He pointed at the bandage covering some sutures. "You took a heavy blow to your head."

"Ask Freddy and Candice," I whispered. "And Andrea."

"Andrea and Wally are the ones who brought you in without mentioning magic doors or ghosts." He patted my hand that lay over my blankets on the hospital bed and stood up. "I think it's lunchtime. What are you having?"

"I don't know," I said, masking my annoyance. "But if it's mashed potatoes again, I'm on strike."

"I'll let the nurses know." He turned to leave, chuckling. I looked up as he grunted and slid past two people outside the door. "Excuse me."

Candice and Freddy walked in, holding hands. The two of them were a sight for my sore, tired eyes. "How are you doing, Delilah?" Freddy asked.

"They don't believe me about what we saw, but I don't blame them. I know I wouldn't either if I were them." I squinted at Candice. "They aren't keeping you?"

She shook her head and looked up at her husband with apprehension in her eyes. Freddy let her hand go and pulled her close, giving her a kiss on her temple. "Go ahead, sweetheart."

"I'm going to be seen in the outpatient program for a while, but I'm not presenting as a risk. Freddy got clearance to work from home for a while."

"I see. Will you come have your lunches with me?"

"About that," Freddy said, taking the seat the doctor vacated minutes before. "Tilly's boys swung by when you were sleeping. They asked if I could talk to you about them staying with you to get you home."

"Patrick is a home care nurse," Candice added, trying to sound helpful.

"Well, that's nice of them. I won't argue if it'll get me out of here."

"It should."

"Finally, some good news." I slammed my head against my pillow, wincing when I felt my head wound throb. "I'm so sick of mashed potatoes."

"So we heard." Freddy sat in the chair beside my bed, pulling Candice into his lap. "There is one more thing we want to tell you."

I turned my head to see Candice rummaging in her purse. "What's that?"

Candice huffed in relief when she found a square piece of paper, no bigger than her hand. She held it out to me. "We are going to be three."

Freddy winked as my brows slammed down over my eyes. As soon as I saw the image on the page, my jaw dropped. "A baby!"

"A little girl!" they both said in unison. Candice blushed, and after a slight nod from Freddy, she added, "We're going to name her Matilda."

"Matilda... Oh! Tilly!" Tears started stinging my eyes.

The two of them hugged me, and they stayed until my lunch arrived. Candice told me Rodrick's strange hobby was not a hobby at all. His fear drove him to dip into dark magic after almost losing the love of his life. He crafted the paint he used to trap Tilly in the room overlooking the pond she loved so she could never leave him. Every ten years, she found the strength to make her presence known, begging her selfish husband to set her free. He declined each time. The year Andrea sent him to the hospital, he realized could no longer hold a paintbrush. His children hated him after years of watching him go mad, so he didn't know anyone who could break his spell. His grief caused him to go mad, and Old Raving Rodrick died feeling guilty for what he did to his wife.

Candice set my best friend free and honored her in the sweetest way possible. It gave me peace, and I went home a few days later. I never found out what happened to Tilly after that night, but I had the feeling the two of us would have tea someday soon.

How Guinevere Met Arthur

Guinevere dashes through the chaotic village streets, her auburn hair flying behind her as she shepherds a group of frightened villagers to safety. "Quickly, this way!" she calls out, her voice cutting through the din of distant clashes and crackling flames. She guides an elderly couple, their faces lined with worry, and a young mother clutching her wailing infant, towards the sturdy stone walls of the village keep.

All around them, the town soldiers move with purpose and determination, their swords glinting in the fading light and their shields held high. They fan out through the narrow alleys and along the cobblestone paths, eyes scanning for any sign of the invaders who have terrorized their village for too long.

The scent of smoke drifts on the evening breeze, carrying with it the acrid tang of burning thatch from the scattered fires left in the wake of the latest attack.

Those not fighting remain in the keep. The soldiers and her father, the village governor, actively fight the onslaught while Guinevere protects their people.

As she ushers the last of the villagers into the location below the floor, she hears a small boy call her from the corner of the room. Turning towards him, she sees Ethan, a boy she's cared for many times in the past. "What are you doing? You should be below with your mother and sister? Who's going to help her?"

"I can't, m'Lady Why do they attack us? Why don't they just move into the village with us?"

"Ethan, some people don't find living in a village easy. We'll be fine. Let's get you to your mother."

After ushering him downstairs, she locks the floorboard door and grabs her bow and sword. Unlike many of the young women in the village, she started training alongside her brothers as a young girl. If the barbarians enter the keep, they are going to face a barrage they won't understand. She pulls over a chair, and climbs into the rafters, sliding away from the door, but in a position she can watch it.

Within moments, she's set up to assail anyone attempting to enter the room.

As Guinevere settles into her perch, her bow at the ready and her sword within easy reach, the heavy wooden door to the keep suddenly slams open with a resounding bang. She tenses, drawing back her bowstring in a fluid motion, the arrow aimed squarely at the entrance.

A figure stumbles into the room, his armor glinting in the flickering torchlight. Guinevere's fingers twitch on the bowstring, a hairsbreadth from loosing the arrow, when she recognizes the familiar face of Sir Palamedes, one of her village's most trusted knights.

"M'Lady Guinevere!" Sir Palamedes calls out, his voice tinged with urgency and desperation. "Hold your fire!"

Guinevere lowers her bow, her heart pounding in her chest as she takes in the knight's disheveled appearance and the grim expression etched on his face. She swiftly descends from the rafters, landing gracefully before him.

"Sir Palamedes, what news? Are the invaders gone?" she asks, her voice steady despite the rising sense of unease in her gut.

The knight nods, his helmet clanking softly with the motion. "Aye, m'Lady, the scoundrels have retreated. But..." He hesitates.

"But what, Sir Palamedes? Speak plainly!" Guinevere demands, her grip tightening on her bow.

"They took your father, m'Lady," Sir Palamedes reveals, his voice heavy with emotion. "We fought valiantly, but they overwhelmed us and captured the governor. I'm so sorry, Guinevere."

Guinevere feels her world tilt, her breath catching in her throat as the weight of Sir Palamedes's words sink in. Her father, the pillar of strength and guidance in her life, is now in the clutches of the barbaric invaders. A storm of emotions swirls within her - fear, anger, determination - but she knows she cannot afford to lose herself to them. Her people, her village, and now her father need her more than ever. "We haven't failed him yet, Palamedes. We're going after him."

He nods.

She spins to a step towards the door. After flinging it open, she calls down the stairwell in the floor below, "They're gone. Return to your homes."

Within minutes, the keep floods with people moving from the security to the outside. As they do, Guinevere orders her friend Palamedes to retrieve the soldiers and knights sent by the king. She prepares a place for them to speak.

By half past the hour, four knights sent by the king join the conversation at the table in the back room.

Sir Palamedes and Sir Zayd stand almost shoulder to shoulder. Both are clearly exhausted, and yet neither utters a complaint. Next to them are Sir Cendric, and Sir Alred remained nearby. As they stand, each one is cleaning their weapons.

The door bursts open and Wynfred, Eldwin, and Cyneheim enter with urgency in their steps.

"You don't expect to do this without us, right?" Wynfred pulls her helmet off as she speaks.

Guinevere takes a deep breath, steeling herself as she faces the assembled knights and soldiers in the room. "Tell me everything you know about the attack and my father's capture," she commands, her voice steady and authoritative.

Sir Palamedes steps forward, his armor still bearing the marks of the recent battle. "M'Lady, the invaders struck swiftly and without warning. They seemed to know exactly where to find your father. We fought bravely, but their numbers were too great. In the chaos, they managed to overwhelm us and took the governor captive."

Eldwin, one of the village's most skilled trackers, speaks up. "Guinevere, Cyneheim and I can track the barbarians. We'll find their trail and follow it, gathering information about their whereabouts and numbers."

Cyneheim nods in agreement, his eyes glinting with determination. "We'll leave immediately and send word back to you as soon as we have something to report."

Guinevere nods, gratitude mixing with the worry in her heart. "Thank you, both of you. Your skills will be invaluable in finding my father."

Sir Zayd, his face lined with concern, steps forward. "M'Lady, I fear we may need more help to face this threat. With your permission, I will ride to King Mark of Cornwall and request additional knights to support our village in this time of need."

Guinevere considers his words, weighing the risks and benefits of seeking outside aid. "Very well, Sir Zayd. Ride swiftly and make our case to the king. We'll need all the help we can get."

The others in the room murmur their agreement, a sense of unity and purpose filling the air. Guinevere looks around at the determined faces of her companions, her resolve strengthening.

"We'll depart in an hour," she announces. "Gather your gear and make your preparations. Eldwin and Cyneheim, leave as soon as you're ready. May the gods guide your path."

The two trackers nod, their expressions grim and focused. They slip out of the room, intent on picking up the trail of the barbarians.

Wynfred, Guinevere's closest friend, steps to her side. "I'm with you, Guin," her hand resting on the hilt of her sword. "We'll find your father and make those barbarians pay for what they've done."

Guinevere clasps Wynfred's arm, a silent acknowledgment. Together, they turn to face the assembled knights and soldiers. "Let's bring my father home," Guinevere declares, her voice ringing with determination.

As one, the group rises and files out of the room, their footsteps echoing on the stone floor. Guinevere and Wynfred follow, their heads held high and their hearts filled with a fierce resolve to rescue the governor and protect their village from the menace of these invaders.

As the sun dips below the horizon, painting the sky in hues of orange and pink, Guinevere and her band of knights and soldiers make their way through the dense forest, following the trail left by the trackers, Eldwin and Cyneheim. The air is thick with the scent of pine and the chirping of crickets, a deceptive tranquility that belies the urgency of their mission.

A soft whistle pierces the air, and Guinevere raises her hand, signaling for the group to halt. She scans the trees, her keen eyes searching for the source of the sound. A moment later, Eldwin and Cyneheim seem to materialize from the shadows, their faces etched with a mix of triumph and concern.

"M'Lady," Eldwin begins, his voice low and urgent, "we've found them. The barbarians have set up camp in a clearing just over the ridge. They've got the governor tied up in the center, guarded by at least a dozen men. The others captured are around him."

Cyneheim nods, his brow furrowed. "From what we could see, they're well-armed and on high alert. It won't be easy to get to your father."

Guinevere takes a deep breath, processing the information. Her heart pounds with a mixture of relief and apprehension. "How many in total?" she asks, her voice steady.

"We counted at least sixty," Eldwin replies grimly. "Maybe more hidden in the tents."

Sir Palamedes steps forward, his hand resting on the hilt of his sword. "M'Lady, if I may," he begins, his tone measured and thoughtful. "We should take some time to observe their movements and routines. Learn their weaknesses before we strike. Rushing in blindly could put the governor's life at even greater risk."

Guinevere nods, appreciating the knight's wisdom. "Agreed. We'll set up camp here and take shifts watching the enemy. Eldwin, Cyneheim, lead Sir Palamedes to the edge of their camp. Learn what you can and report back."

As the three men slip back into the forest, Wynfred moves to Guinevere's side, her arms laden with a bundle of sticks and stones. "While we wait," she says, a determined glint in her eye, "Time to start crafting some more arrows. We'll need every advantage we can get."

Guinevere smiles at her friend, grateful for her foresight and skills. Around them, the other soldiers and knights settle in, some tending to their weapons, others speaking in hushed tones about the challenges ahead.

Sir Cendric, a grizzled veteran of many battles, shares his experiences with the barbarian tribe. "I've faced these brutes before," he growls, his fingers tracing the scars on his weathered face. "They're fierce and unpredictable, but they're not invincible. The key is to strike hard and fast, give them no time to regroup."

Sir Alred nods in agreement, his eyes remain distant, as if recalling his own encounters. "They fight without honor," he adds, his voice tinged with disgust. "They'll use every dirty trick in the book to gain the upper hand. We must be prepared for anything."

As the night wears on, Guinevere paces the perimeter of the camp, her mind racing with possibilities and plans. The weight of her father's life hangs heavy on her shoulders, but she refuses to let it crush her spirit.

In the distance, an owl hoots, its eerie cry piercing the stillness of the forest. Guinevere shivers, pulling her cloak tighter around her shoulders. She can feel the eyes of her companions upon her, looking for guidance and strength in this darkest of hours.

Just as the first hints of dawn paints the eastern sky, Eldwin and Cyneheim return with Sir Palamedes, their faces grim and exhausted. They gather around Guinevere, their voices low and urgent as they share what they've learned.

"The barbarians are restless," Eldwin reports, his eyes dark with concern. "They argue amongst themselves, as if debating what to do with the governor. Some want to kill him outright, others want to use him as a bargaining chip."

Cyneheim nods, his jaw clenched tight. "They're heavily armed and well-trained. It won't be an easy fight, even with the element of surprise on our side."

Sir Palamedes rubs his chin thoughtfully, his gaze distant as he weighs their options. "We need to create a diversion," he suggests, his voice low and measured. "Draw their attention away from the governor long enough for a small group to slip in and free him."

Guinevere listens intently, her mind whirling with possibilities. She knows every decision she makes from this point forward could mean the difference between life and death, not just for her father, but for all those who follow her.

As the sun rises higher in the sky, casting dappled shadows through the trees, Guinevere and her companions huddle together, formulating their plan. The air is thick with tension and anticipation, each member of the group acutely aware of the stakes at hand.

Wynfred, her quiver full of expertly crafted arrows, and her field arrows, stands at Guinevere's side. "We're with you, Guin," she says softly, her hand resting on her friend's shoulder. "To the end."

Guinevere nods, drawing strength from the unwavering support of her companions. She knows that the road ahead will be perilous, fraught with danger and uncertainty. She also knows she is not alone, that she has the skill, courage, and loyalty of some of the finest warriors in the land at her back.

Guinevere's thoughts turn to her father, to the man who raised her to be strong, brave, and compassionate. She silently vows to do whatever it takes to bring him home safely, to protect her village and her people from the scourge of the barbarian horde.

The forest seems to hold its breath, the very trees and rocks waiting in hushed anticipation for the battle to come. Guinevere closes her eyes, offering a silent prayer to the gods for strength, guidance, and victory in the face of overwhelming odds.

In hushed tones, they decide on a distraction. This will take all the strength she has, and the timing must be right. She trusts those with her. They object to the idea but trust her nonetheless.

Once the choices are settled, she stands, pulls her hood over her head, and tosses Wynfred her bow and quiver. "I'll see you all in the camp."

Guinevere spins on her heel, and marches around the field to the far side, out of sight of her allies. She then turns towards the ridge. Up and over within thirty minutes, she marches towards the camp, ignoring the troops trying to approach her.

At the edge of the camp, Guinevere pauses, her eyes scanning the scene before her. Tents of various sizes and colors dot the clearing. Hides adorned with intricate patterns and symbols. The scent of smoke and roasting meat wafts through the air, mingling with the pungent odor of unwashed bodies and horse sweat. Throughout the camp, barbarian warriors, both men and women, go about their morning routines, sharpening weapons, tending to fires, and preparing for the day ahead.

Taking a deep breath, Guinevere steps into the camp, her head held high, and her gaze fixed. Almost immediately, the nearest barbarians take notice of her presence, their eyes widening in surprise and their hands instinctively reaching for their weapons. She ignores their hostile stares and continues forward, her steps measured and purposeful.

"I demand to speak with your chief," Guinevere calls out, her voice ringing clear and strong across the camp. "I have a proposal."

A ripple of murmurs and whispers spreads through the gathered barbarians, their expressions ranging from curiosity to outright suspicion. After a moment of tense silence, a large, burly man emerges from the largest tent, his bare chest adorned with intricate tattoos and his long, braided hair adorned with beads and feathers. He strides towards Guinevere, his eyes narrowing as he takes in her appearance.

"I am Rothgar, chief of the Bear Clan," he growls, his voice deep and guttural. "What business do you have here, woman?"

Guinevere meets his gaze unflinchingly. Her chin lifted in defiance. "I am Guinevere, daughter of the governor of Effinheim. I come to offer myself in exchange for his freedom."

A chorus of laughter erupts from the gathered barbarians, their mocking tones filling the air. Rothgar himself lets out a bark of amusement, his eyes glinting with a mixture of incredulity and disdain. "And why should I accept such a trade?" he asks, his tone dripping with sarcasm. "What value does a mere woman hold compared to a fierce ruler?"

Guinevere's eyes flash with indignation, but she maintains her composure. "I am no mere woman," she retorts, her voice steady and strong. "I am a skilled warrior, trained in the art of combat since childhood. As his child, I am also the heir to my father's lands and title. By taking me, you gain not only a valuable hostage, but also a key to the riches and power of our kingdom."

Rothgar's brow furrows as he considers her words, his gaze sweeping over her form appraisingly. Around them, the barbarians mutter amongst themselves, some nodding in agreement while others scoff at the notion of a woman warrior.

"Pretty words," Rothgar finally says, his tone still skeptical. "But how do I know you speak the truth? How do I know you won't try to escape the moment your father is freed?"

Guinevere takes a step closer to the chief, her eyes locked with his. "I give you my word as a noble of the realm," she says, her voice ringing with conviction. "I will accept my father's place as your captive, and I will not attempt to flee. You have my honor as a warrior and a daughter."

Rothgar's eyes narrow, his gaze boring into hers as if trying to discern any hint of deception. Guinevere meets his stare unflinchingly, her own expression focused with determination and sincerity.

For a long moment, the two remain locked in this silent battle of wills, the tension in the air palpable. Around them, the barbarians watch with bated breath, their hands tightening on their weapons as they await their chief's decision.

Finally, Rothgar speaks, his voice low and measured. "You claim to be a skilled warrior," he says, his tone still laced with doubt. "Prove it. Fight one of my champions, and if you emerge victorious, I will accept your offer."

Guinevere's heart skips a beat at the challenge. She knows this may be her only chance to save her father and the captive people. With a curt nod, she accepts the chief's terms.

A murmur of excitement ripples through the gathered barbarians, and Rothgar barks out an order in their guttural language. Within moments, a hulking brute of a man steps forward, his massive frame rippling with muscle and his face etched with a cruel grin.

Guinevere sizes up her opponent, noting his broad shoulders, thick neck, and the wicked-looking axe he wields with ease. She knows this will be no easy fight, but she also knows she has the speed, agility, and training to overcome his brute strength.

As the two warriors face off in the center of the camp, the barbarians form a circle around them, their eyes gleaming with anticipation. Guinevere draws her sword from its sheath, the blade glinting in the morning light. She settles into a fighting stance, her feet planted firmly on the ground and her body coiled like a spring, ready to strike.

The barbarian champion lets out a bellowing war cry and charges forward, his axe raised high above his head. Guinevere waits until the last possible moment before darting to the side, her sword slashing out to score a shallow cut along the brute's arm.

The barbarian roars in pain. His eyes reflect his fury as he whirls to face her once more. Guinevere dances back, her sword at the ready, her heart pounding, anticipating his next move.

The fight is brutal and merciless, the clang of steel against steel ringing out across the camp as the two trade blows. Guinevere's speed and agility serve her well, allowing her to evade the barbarian's powerful strikes and land with her own slashes and thrusts.

Unfortunately, the barbarian is a formidable opponent, his strength and endurance seemingly inexhaustible. Guinevere's energy flags as the minutes drag on. Her arms grow heavy and her breath comes in ragged heaves.

Just as the barbarian might overwhelm her, Guinevere strikes an opening. With a desperate lunge, she drives her sword deep into brute's leg, sending him crumpling to the ground. As the red, rapidly swelling wound forms clearly in his thigh, she steps back from him and out of the battle. Determination pushes her to remain not far away, waiting for the response.

A stunned silence falls over the camp as the barbarians stare in disbelief at their fallen champion. Guinevere stands near his body, her chest heaving and her sword smeared with blood.

Slowly, Rothgar steps forward, his expression unreadable as he surveys the scene. For a long moment, he says nothing, his gaze flickering between Guinevere and the fallen warrior at her feet. When he speaks, his voice is low and grudging. "You have proven your worth, woman," he says, his tone laced with a reluctant respect. "I will consider your offer of exchange."

Guinevere nods

As Rothgar turns to confer with his advisors, Guinevere catches a flicker of movement out of the corner of her eye. She turns her head slightly. Her gaze draws to the edge of the camp, where a familiar figure lurks.

Sir Palamedes meets her gaze for a fleeting instant that shares volumes with her. Guinevere gives a barely perceptible nod, acknowledging his presence and the unspoken plan they have set in motion.

It is a risky gambit, one that could easily backfire if the barbarians were to discover their presence too soon. Guinevere has faith in her people, in their courage, and in their cunning.

Restlessness is evident among the barbarians. People gather weapons, clean them or begin packing. Some move to put out fires, while others begin pacing around a tent with clearly established guards. All indications tell her things will turn against her soon.

A sudden commotion erupts from the far side of the camp. Shouts of alarm alert everyone to the pounding of hooves as a herd of horses thunders through the tents. As Guinevere's gaze darts from one to the next, she notes their eyes are wide with panic.

The barbarians scatter, some reaching for their weapons while others dive out of the way of the stampeding animals. Amid the chaos, Guinevere glimpses a familiar figure emerging from one tent, his face haggard but his eyes alight with fierce joy.

"Father!" she cries out. Her heart leaps in her chest as she realizes her people have succeeded in their mission.

The governor stumbles forward, supported by Sir Cendric and Sir Alred. Their swords flashing in the sun as they cut down any barbarians who try to stop them. Behind them, a small group of freed captives emerge, their faces pale but determined as they make their bid for freedom. Some pull the swords from fallen barbarians and engage the battle as they move from the chaos.

Guinevere wastes no time seizing the opportunity presented by the horses. She spots an incoming steed. Pacing her steps to remotely catch the horse, she prepares herself. Once alongside the animal, her hands weave into the mane. With a swift, fluid motion, she leaps onto the back, her fingers hold firmly to its mane as she urges it forward.

The horse responds to her touch, its hooves pounding against the ground as it surges towards the edge of the camp. Guinevere leans low over its neck, her cloak streaming behind her as she navigates through the mass of panicked barbarians and stampeding horses.

As she rides past, she catches a last glimpse of Rothgar's face, witnessing a mix of rage and disbelief as he realizes he has been outmaneuvered. Guinevere doesn't savor the victory.

Her only thought is of her father, of the need to get him and the other captives to safety as quickly as possible. She urges her horse onward, her heart pounding in time with its hoofbeats as they race towards the edge of the forest.

Behind her, she can hear the shouts and curses of the barbarians as they give chase, their own horses pounding against the earth as they try to overtake her. Guinevere moves in perfect harmony with her mount as she weaves through the trees and underbrush.

She watches her team navigate around her, gathering in a stream of riders racing for the village. She finds herself just behind the last of the captives and soldiers, alongside the most trusted knights of the village.

As Guinevere races through the village gates, the heavy wooden doors slam shut behind her with a resounding thud. The sound echoes through the narrow streets and alleyways. She reins in her horse, its hooves skidding on the cobblestones as it comes to a halt in the center of the square.

Around her, the village is a flurry of activity, with people rushing to and fro. Their faces show a mixture of relief and joy at the sight of their returning heroes. The rescue team, led by Sir Palamedes and Sir Cendric, ride in just behind Guinevere, their faces flushed with the thrill of victory.

At the center of the group is the governor, his head held high and his eyes shining with pride and gratitude. Despite the ordeal, he appears unharmed, his bearing remains as regal and commanding as ever. As they approach, Guinevere notes how he continues to speak with the previous captives as freely as he does family.

As Guinevere dismounts and rushes to her father's side, he envelops her in a fierce embrace. He murmurs words of appreciation in her ear. Guinevere clings to him, with relief and happiness overcoming her because he is safe and home.

Around them, the rescued soldiers are in high spirits. The air is filled with laughter and chatter as the soldiers are reunited with their families and friends. Many of them bear the marks of their captivity, with bruises and scrapes pocking their skin. Despite this, the brief captivity seems to melt away among family.

Sir Alred, one of the younger knights, leaps from his horse and throws his arms around his wife, lifting her off the ground as he spins her in a circle, their laughter mingling with the joyful tears streaming down their faces. Nearby, Sir Cendric embraces his elderly mother.

The rescue team, too, is caught up in the celebratory mood, with Sir Palamedes and Sir Ellsworth clasping hands and grinning broadly at each other, a demonstration of mutual respect and celebration between a pair of typically reserved knights.

Guinevere takes a step back. She knows this victory would not have been possible without the bravery and dedication of her knights and soldiers, even the fallen. She silently vows to honor their sacrifice in every way she can. As she turns to face her companions, Guinevere is met with a sea of smiling faces. The knights and soldiers alike rush forward to offer their congratulations and praise.

Sir Palamedes takes her hand in his. He bows deeply before her. "Lady Guinevere," he says, his voice ringing out clear and strong across the square, "your courage saved your father and the captives. You are truly a courageous woman."

Guinevere feels a flush as he speaks, but before she responds, a sudden commotion at the gates draws her attention. She turns to see a young watchman racing towards them, his face pale and his eyes wide.

"My lady!" he gasps, skidding to a halt before her, his chest heaving with exertion. "The barbarian chief is at the gates, with two of his men. They are calling for the warrior woman who walked into their camp."

A hush falls over the crowd. The joyful chatter gives way to an uneasy silence. Guinevere feels an icy knot of dread forming in the pit of her stomach. She's aware of her place and forces herself to remain calm. "I'll go," she says, her voice steady and strong as she turns to face her father and her knights. "I will hear what they have to say."

"Guinevere, no!" her father speaks sternly. "You cannot trust these savages."

Sir Palamedes steps forward, his hand resting on the hilt of his sword. "My lady, allow us to accompany you," he says, his voice low and urgent. "We cannot let you face them alone."

Guinevere shakes her head, her jaw set with determination. "No, Sir Palamedes," she says, her voice brooking no argument. "I am only going to speak to them from the gate."

"Very well," the governor responds at last, his voice heavy with resignation. "But be careful. Remember that you are the heart and soul of this village."

Guinevere nods, a small smile tugging at the corners of her lips. "I will, Father."

As she strides towards the wall, her head remains high and her steps are purposeful. Guinevere can feel the eyes of her people upon her. No matter what Rothgar wants, she knows she cannot let them down.

At the top of the wall, she looks down at the barbarian chief and his men, her eyes narrowing as she does. Rothgar rests on his steed at the center, his massive frame clad in furs and his eyes glinting with a mixture of anger and perhaps grudging respect.

"What do you want?" Guinevere calls down, ringing out loud and clear across the distance between them.

Rothgar ushers his steed forward, his gaze locked with hers as he speaks. "You have another challenge, woman," he says, his voice a low, menacing growl.

Guinevere feels a flicker of surprise at his words, but she quickly masks it with a look of cool, unwavering confidence. She responds in a dismissive tone, "I'm ready for whatever challenge you bring."

At her words, one barbarian, a hulking brute of a man with a scar running down the length of his face, steps forward. "I am Brokk, champion of the Bear Clan," he says, his voice a guttural, rasping growl. "I challenge you to a fight, woman. Your honor depends on it."

Guinevere meets his gaze. "My honor does not depend on it. I do not need to accept further challenges "

Rothgar watches the exchange with a calculating gaze, his eyes flickering between Guinevere and his champion with a look of shrewd appraisal. Finally, he speaks, his voice low and measured as he addresses the warrior woman before him.

"You like making deals, woman," he says, his tone almost conversational. "So let us make a deal now. If you defeat Brokk in single combat, the Bear Clan will never again raid this village or its people. You have my word as a chief and a warrior."

Guinevere feels a sudden rush of excitement at his words, her heart pounding with the thrill of the challenge and the promise of a lasting peace for her people. She knows this is an opportunity she cannot afford to pass up, a chance to secure the safety of her village.

"And if I lose?"

"You become the wife of Brokk. As such, it will merge your village with our clan. Your village remains safe."

"You want me to believe my people will win no matter how this battle ends?"

"If you can handle the challenge."

She knows Rothgar is not a man to be trusted lightly, that his word is only as good as the strength of his own honor and the sharpness of his blade. Guinevere lifts her chin to face the barbarian chief once more, her voice steady and strong as she speaks the words that will seal their fate.

"I accept your challenge and your terms, Rothgar of the Bear Clan," she says, her gaze unwavering. "But know this: if I defeat your champion, you will keep your word, or you will face the full might of my people and my allies. This is a promise, from one warrior to another."

Rothgar's eyes narrow at her words, but there is a glint of something like respect in his gaze as he nods slowly, his massive frame shifting slightly as he regards the woman before him. "So be it," he says, his voice a low, rumbling growl that seems to echo across the valley. "We have agreed upon the terms, and the challenge is set. Prepare yourself, Guinevere of Effinheim. The fight begins at first light."

With those final words, the barbarian chief turns and rides away, his champion and his men falling in behind him as they disappear into the mists beyond the village walls. Guinevere watches them go.

A few moments pass before she moves back to her father and the knights with him. Guinevere feels a sense of calm and purpose settling over her, a quiet certainty she will emerge victorious, no matter the odds or the obstacles that stand in her way.

At the first light of dawn breaking over the horizon, painting the sky in a breathtaking array of pinks and golds, Guinevere emerges from her chambers. Her armor gleams in the early morning light. Her face is a mask of determination, her eyes blazing with a fierce, unyielding resolve as she strides towards the stables, her cloak flowing behind her in the gentle breeze.

At her side walks Wynfred, her closest friend and confidante, her own armor polished to a high shine and her sword resting comfortably at her hip. The two women exchange a look of quiet understanding as they approach their waiting horses, their bond forged through countless shared experiences.

"Are you ready for this?" Wynfred asks softly, her voice tinged with concern as she helps Guinevere mount her steed, a magnificent black stallion.

Guinevere nods, her jaw set with determination as she settles into the saddle, her hands gripping the reins with a sure, steady strength. "I am," she says, her voice ringing out clear and strong in the early morning air. "I won't let our people down."

Wynfred swings herself up onto her own horse, a sleek chestnut mare with a fiery spirit. She guides her mount alongside Guinevere's, their hooves kicking up a fine spray of dust as they set off towards the village gates.

As they ride, Wynfred turns to Guinevere, a mischievous glint in her eye. "Are you ready to become the wife of that brute, Brokk?" she asks, her voice dripping with sarcasm. "I hear he has a lovely collection of animal skulls decorating his tent."

Guinevere throws back her head with laughter, the sound ringing out like a bell in the morning's stillness. "Oh, absolutely," she says, her voice laced with mock sincerity. "I can hardly wait to spend my days cooking his meals and mending his furs. It's every girl's dream come true."

The two women dissolve into laughter, as they imagine the absurdity of Guinevere as a barbarian's wife. They both know that she would sooner die than submit to such a fate, her spirit too wild and untamed to ever break.

As they approach the designated meeting spot, a wide, open field just beyond the village walls, Guinevere and Wynfred's laughter fades. Their expressions grow serious and focused once more. They can see Rothgar and Brokk waiting for them, their massive frames dwarfing their own horses as they sit astride their battle-hardened steeds.

Guinevere and Wynfred draw their horses to a halt a few paces away from the barbarians, their eyes locked on their opponents with unwavering intensity. Rothgar leans forward in his saddle, his gaze sweeping over Guinevere with a mixture of curiosity and respect.

"Greetings, Guinevere of Effinheim," he says, his voice a low, rumbling growl that seems to echo across the field. "I trust you are prepared for the challenge ahead."

Guinevere inclines her head, her eyes never leaving Rothgar's face. "I am," her voice steady and strong.

Rothgar nods, his expression unreadable as he recites the terms of their bargain. "If you defeat Brokk in single combat, the Bear Clan will never again raid your village or your people. If you lose, you will become his wife, and your village will be merged with our people, under our protection."

Guinevere nods, her jaw tight. "And there will be no interference from either side," she says, her voice ringing out clear and firm. "Skill and strength alone will decide this fight, with no trickery or deception."

Rothgar's eyes narrow, but he nods his assent, his massive frame shifting slightly in the saddle. "Agreed," he says, his voice a low, menacing growl. "Let the challenge begin."

With those words, Guinevere and Wynfred dismount their horses, their movements fluid and graceful as they hand the reins to a waiting attendant.

"Fight well, my friend," she says, her voice low and intense. "Show them your strength."

Guinevere nods, a small smile tugging at the corners of her lips. "I will," she says, her voice a whisper that seems to carry across the field.

She turns back towards Brokk. Her gaze narrows. Her mind wanders to the fight the day before. Both this one and that, she's up against a much larger opponent. Her attempt to take the champion head on in her last match almost didn't work. She's determined not to repeat that mistake.

She steps towards the warrior ahead of her. She watches the way he moves around a circle. He's like a predator looking for the moment to pounce.

She matches his movements with lighter nibble steps. She easily dodges his first lunge and his second. He brings his axe towards her, but she slides away from it. So far, so good.

Each time Brokk tries to close the gap, she extends it. Every time his battle axe swings she moves out of the path. After the fourth or fifth attempt, he changes his process. An arm juts out to grab her mid-dodge. Caught by one hand, Guinevere pivots away, clearly aware that won't happen again.

She flips her sword, like she used to in practice. It is a telling, nervous habit she hopes he picks up on. Her hand slides back under her armor as he charges. This time, she doesn't move. Her sword lifts, her dagger in hand now. He pivots away from the sword, and she plunges the dagger into his shoulder.

It worked! Inside, Guinevere squeals at her success. Outwardly, she remains composed. It isn't enough to stop him, but it's a good start.

They resume their cat mouse pacing around the ring.

He charges, she dodges. He slashes. She steps away. This continues until she can get behind him. This time, his sound battle axe first. Even flailing wildly, he nearly strikes her.

"How do you expect to marry me if you take my head off?" She spins out of his way.

He chuckles.

After a few more minutes of this, Brokk slams the axe into the ground. Now minimally armed, he places both hands in the air.

"Aww, are you surrendering now?" Guinevere doesn't realize she let her guard down until he moves swifter than she's seen him do so far, grabbing her in the process.

Pulled against his chest, she struggles in his grip. At that moment, she wishes she still held her dagger. When he forces the sword to fall, there's no doubt she's in trouble. Struggling, wiggling, and flailing does little more than upset Brokk.

To better contain her, Brokk lifts the woman from the ground. This is where Guinevere takes her chance. As her feet leave the ground, her boots slam hard into his personal regions.

They both collapse to the ground.

She's fast to clamor for her sword and is standing again before he is.

She presses the blade against his abdomen. "Yield."

With tears welling from the pain, Brokk refuses. He rolls to his side.

Guinevere kicks him hard, then brings her sword down on his arm. "Yield."

He staggers to his feet. Once he's standing, his eyes search for his battle axe. Guinevere stands between him and the weapon.

She levels her sword. "Do not force more. You are defeated."

Briefly, she focuses her attention on Sir Zaryd and a line of knights accompanying him.

Brokk charges. Guinevere lifts the sword, but he knocks it from her grasp. She slams her heel into his groin before he can do more than grab her. This time, the force used causes him to cry out as he crumbles.

She picks up her sword and puts it in her sheath. Turning to Rothgar, she declares, "He can no longer fight. The battle is won. Safe travels."

She moves swiftly to her horse, Wynfred falls into line with her steps. Within moments, they are in the saddles again.

The women bring their horses alongside Sir Zayd. "It is good to see you again, my friend."

Sir Zayd nods. "M'Lady." He gazes towards Rothgar and Brokk as they are gathering themselves to leave. "It seems we arrived far too late to be of use."

"Not at all, Zayd." Wynfred grins. "You arrived right on time. Witness the victory of our Lady against the Bear Clan, saving our village from further attack."

The knights with Zayd smirk and share glances. Zayd gives them a quick glance. "M'Lady, allow me to introduce the knights dispatched to assist." He gestures to his right. "While these are newly knighted young men, each one has proven themselves," Zayd states. The first is Lancelot. He is, much like you, the son of a town head. His valor is unmatched."

Lancelot removes his helmet as Zayd speaks. "It is a pleasure to meet you, m'Lady."

Zayd continues introductions. "Next to him is Sir Tristan and Sir Bedivere." The men also remove their helmets and greet Guinevere and Wynfred.

Before an introduction can be made for him, the next knight speaks up, "It is a pleasure to see how becoming armor can be on such a beautiful lady."

With a slight groan, Zayd explains, "Lord Charming is Sir Gawain." He shakes his head. "Their selected commander is on the far end." Zayd gestures to the man without a helmet, astride an ebony steed. "He is Arthur."

4:15 GALACTIC STANDARD EXPRESS

T hanks to the memory enhancers nestled in the nodes behind my left ear, even though the events I'm about to tell you about took place nine years, three months, and five days ago, I can still remember everything clearly.

As like all afternoons in space, there was no weather to distract a being's gaze, only eternal darkness from one side of the ship, and a muddle of earthy colors seen when gazing down at the full-colored glory of Zilia 5F1. It was one of the smallest planets in the region and, unfortunately, only accessible by space shuttle; I had arranged to leave Planetary Station Creon and be on the 4:15 GS express to Port Station Exclite, disembarking at Port Station Tilara. As usual, since I dabbled in engineering when I was young (before being forced to acknowledge that I had no talent for it), I took the remaining time dregs of my early arrival to examine the ship in her berth.

She was a beauty. Even I could see that. A dull silver contradictorily bright and bold in the brilliant lights of the station. A unique limited edition gave her an old-fashioned covering. She was, of course, part of an old company which liked to brag about keeping to their Earthian roots. The past was clear to see on her, and in the lobby had meant putting up old maps, making fake travel flyers to "nearby" planets. Gamble on Mercury, pamper yourself on Venus, and propose to your sweetheart amid the rings of Saturn!

It was a prideful love, and the changes extended to the space shuttle as well. Like any other shuttle it had a nose in front, but beyond that there were nods to a very well loved transportation form the company began with; the train.

There were dim lights on the outside with faux lanterns painted around them, handles that never moved since the doors automatically closed, and, to my delight, there were several individual compartments inside, some of which were private for a modest fee and a bit of luck. Most shuttles had done away from such trivial frivolities, preferring to go the traditional route of more beings in the seats equalling more credits in the bank.

With a lightness to my stride that I attributed to the lower gravity on the platform, I stepped onto the ramp, passed through the doorway, and found the guard. As usual with private transportation, the inside drove away any lingering thoughts of space's unyielding deepness—it was always better for space travelers not to succumb to kenophobia.

The atmosphere now was of dark hardwood on the floor, gold burnished and gleaming cleanly around me. Old fashioned hat/trench coat uniforms. And when I say "old" I was talking about centuries, at this point, which had me making a mental note to invite my anthropologist friend along on my next ride. She would either find everything amusing and get a good laugh out of it, or she would go nigh apocalyptic telling me just how every detail wasn't quite right.

Debating if I should keep that mental note or delete it. I distracted myself by questioning the guard if any of the private carriages were open, and with my luck shining high, was directed to the final section of the shuttle. A small keypad ensured I would be locked in for the duration of the trip, which was completely fine by me. Each area had several configurations to be conducive to whatever activity was wanted; sleeping, reading, drinking, eating, etc. The floor was currently in a neutral phase of carpet, though the material could switch as easily as the need.

It was here that I took Niffle out of its small cage, encouraged it to glow, then pulled out my tablet to keep reading. It was a wonderful book about betrayal, trust, and how dangerous trying to piece together broken slivers could be. The lovely tale had been given to me by the previously mentioned anthropologist friend.

So my disappointment was great when, not even two minutes before departure, another being opened the locked door with a private key and entered the carriage. I bit my tongue even though I was annoyed. It was possible there was no other seat open, and this was the most spacious of all the carriages. Truthfully, there were plenty of stations which we would be heading toward in the near future. I might not need to share this space for long.

As I peered at the new addition, it struck me that I had seen this being before. A rarity some might say when they think about how large space is. Others might comment how inevitable it would be as all being trod common roads.

In this instance, they carried themselves well, balancing on three of their four legs as they turned around. A long, snapping black tail ending with a tuft of red hair, a half-kilt over their backside (a gesture not needed on their own planet, but which most of their kind adopted when they were in the presence of two-legged beings such as myself). And finally, they turned enough that I could glimpse their faces, and in that there was no mistaking.

Long red, white, and black hair grew in spurts of roughness from their mane, they had a polished gold piercing hooped through their nostrils, and as those flared, their eyes widened, showing me one white eye long-since scared over and the other a warm black. Thin-lipped and starry eyed, with a gracefulness I'd only seen from smaller Earth animals, they triple circled the small area between us, then laid their whole feline body lengthwise across the seat, all four feet hanging above the floor in what looked like a slide halted in mid motion.

They lightly touched one side of the pockets slung over their hindquarters, took a tablet out from another pocket, and glanced at me only once as they began reading. I didn't mind. It gave me a few more moments to be certain that I truly recognized them as sometimes memory enhancers weren't accurate.

An assortment of other items about their person included a portable biometric safe, which they had stored overhead before laying on the seat, a small communications tablet which was placed on the small table between us, and finally, a vacuum packed blanket which enlarged to nestle over their larger feline-centaured body.

Everything done to their satisfaction, they leaned over to the drink provider and dialed up something that assaulted my nose with its strong fumes.

"Apologies," they said in a low voice. "I'll make sure to drink this quickly. I can see by your wrinkled nose that it doesn't agree with your biology."

"No apologies needed," I said, feeling the spaceship start moving. To be more precise, I saw through the window that we were leaving the berth for the starspace beyond, and the human brain automatically translated that "feeling" into action even when it couldn't be felt. When this company advertised smooth flights, it certainly lived up to its promise.

I had recognized my companion before, truly, identifying xem by their red-dipped tail, and the most beautiful starry eyes I'd ever seen on a being. It just took a few moments for xyr name to pop up; Nakvoir. Xe was a geneticist by profession, and I recalled a tangible thread between xem and the woman whom I was traveling to meet (xe was her lover's kin).

I looked to xem again, with a keener eye, and noticed that xe was raggedy, as if xyr fur hadn't been brushed in days, or worse, was in danger of falling out due to stress. There was a restlessness to xyr legs. I saw at least three separate twitches as I observed xem, and, though I wasn't around enough Lodiers (xyr species) to know for certain, it seemed as if there was a hollow look about xyr face. On a human I would have guessed sickness or grief. In the three years between meetings, life, it seemed, had not done well for xem.

Xe was most likely bound for the same stop as I, if we were both on a path to meet up with Mrs. Ginerva. I was looking forward to a women's night of sharing the newest facts and discoveries from my station, along with a delightful lay-in for the morning, followed by a very old-fashioned British tea in the afternoon. Imagining what delights awaited me, I could already feel my mouth watering at clotted cream and scones.

Mrs. Ginerva (and she was insistent upon the pre-name moniker) was one of those beings for whom monogamy didn't work, and a current partner of hers was similar in physique to Nakvoir—of course, as soon as I remembered this, my enchanters drew upon the faint threads in my brain. I distinctly recalled that they were beings of the same clan (sharing an ancestor a few generations back), though Nakvoir had a higher standing in society due to xyr job in genetics. My friend's paramour, the last I'd heard, had no such measurable job, and was therefore found wanting.

Xe had glanced at me as xe'd fixed xyr drink, but without a hint of recollection or recognition. Now, after slamming down whatever strong drink xe polluted the air with, xe looked over me again, a doubtful appearance in xyr one working eye. It was only when xe obviously did so for the fourth or fifth time that I decided to speak and release xem from the fog of déjà vu and half-forgotten reminiscences found tattered in the morning light.

"Nakvoir of Red Light, I think?

"That is my name and my clan," he replied, eyebrows furrowing. "And yet, I cannot place yours."

"I met you and your kin at Mrs. Ginevra's party three years ago," I said, throwing xem a lifeline. "The one she threw as a celebration when pineapples became imports again."

"Ah, the fruit with the acid that digests your tongue. With a pleasant flavor inticiting the behavior."

"Yes."

"I thought I knew your scent," xe said; "my memory, however, was not—"

"No worries at all. Rolife—Rolife Ann. I've known Mrs. Ginevra since we were studying together in the miniscule Space Station #19 school. When I come this way to take care of other errands, I find the pull to her house magnetic. Perhaps, the same might be said for you?" I smiled and leaned back against the cushion. "I can only assume we're for the same stop."

"Not if you're on your way to meet with her," xe replied. "I am traveling on business—rather anncying business, to be honest—while if you are meeting up with the gracious Ginevra, then you doubtless have only pleasures awaiting."

I blushed at the thought of the pleasures xe might be thinking of, and was quick to describe an itinerary of the weekend's activities.

"Truly," I added at the end, "I'm in the habit of seeing any visit with her as being the most joyous time cn my calendar, no matter the season."

"She keeps her house, and herself, pleasant." Xe grinned. "I'm glad my kin was able to find her in this life, and I wish them luck in growing the family."

"The pleasantest person I know," I agreed. "Even if I don't know when, where, or who she learned that."

Life aboard a space station doesn't lend itself well to being free with food, water, or space. I'd always thought it was possible for one to develop anti-feelings from childhood and Mrs. Ginevra was, in my opinion, life's unofficial confirmation of my idea.

"She has invited me to spend the next few weeks with her and my kin. A mixed celebration of my clan's day of remembrance and the old Earth custom called 'Christmas'?"

I snorted, and xe gave me a quizzical look.

"While Christmas started as a religious gathering, I believe you've hit exactly upon how Ginevra likes to celebrate it; secular. Pretty lights, good food, presents. Will you be joining?"

"If nothing else changes, then it's a possibility. As of right now, I cannot tell."

"Business?"

Xe nodded, ther selected another drink from the menu. "I can understand if you have not, but have you perhaps heard of the Blank Gene?"

I drew in a quick breath. "Blank Gene. The Blank Gene? Such as the 'gene' that can copy any phenotype and insert the needed balance of genetic information into anyone's DNA—that 'Blank Gene'?"

"I did not take you for a geneticist."

"I am but a marketer, but one of my co-workers is a true scientist, and he's been telling all of us about this remarkable development." I narrowed my eyes. "The last he'd heard, however, was that the Blank Gene wasn't fully guaranteed."

"And he is correct. I'm bringing it with me to a secret lab to decrease its number of shortcomings."

I explained that I'd heard nothing about specific shortcomings from my colleague, and xe smiled wryly.

"It does a company no good if their worst is being whispered and bandied about. By the time rumors are quieted in one area of the galaxy, they're rampant in another. In this case though, it will have an improvement. A great improvement, which will become an important part of communication, negotiations, and more! Imagine it—making full use of body parts not found normally in your natural physical state to speak second, or even third languages. I was the one to see the potential in collaborating with the Diplomatic Corp."

I could tell xe was getting excited, xyr tail swishing back and forth.

"People could only see this being used for bad, or at best, for the genetic-cosmetic market. A market that goes up and down depending on people's interests. Our own marketing department said the Blank Gene would last about ten, maybe eleven years before the desire goes down. But with my course of action, we'll go beyond that downward spiral and make the best of it with foreign language communication!"

"That makes you part of the staff at Geneki."

"Yes." Xe settled back down on the seat again, and I saw xem check to make sure xe hadn't accidentally clawed anything in xyr fervor. "My interest in the company is threefold. First, I myself am a geneticist. Second, I am a considerable shareholder since I joined the company when it first started and the credit flow was very narrow. And finally, third, I've attained board of directors status."

Then, since I'd clearly shown interest in xem and all three titles xe held, Nakvoir continued to tell me all the pressing details on xyr mind, in xyr heart, and conjured up by his excited spirit. I was "entertained" with a multitude of key people, secret deals, complaints, and more details than I'd ever wanted to know.

For instance, there had been a number of beings opposing Blank Gene. People were worried it would be used for crimes, others wanted a bigger cut of the proceeds, a single being wanted their name first of the paper, therefore giving her larger dividends.

At least those motivations I could understand. When xe moved into the precise intricacies of how xe planned to make changes to the Blank Gene's make, I could only nod and smile in accordance with what I saw in xyr physique. Xe laid everything out before me, leaving not a star unobserved.

When xe stopped to break for yet another drink, and to capture the amount of oxygen needed for further conversation, I wasn't able to leave. Somehow, with technology high enough to resemble magic, I presume, xe managed to dive deeper. Now the conversation was less about marketing, which I might have followed with a bare glimmer of understanding, and more about the business side, which unfortunately didn't follow down the sales path (to which I could have added information as I was in marketing and sales).

In spite of grabbing myself a double espresso coffee from the menu, I could feel myself nodding off, no matter how much I pried my eyes open enough to show I was paying attention. From the dull details I was given, it seemed everyone was against this amazing piece of technology, or they wanted to appropriate it for misuse.

One religious group wanted to create their savior in the living flesh. Another company imagined they'd be ruined—they sold genetic modifications on the market and felt they could compete with this. There was even a poison pen letter (imagine receiving paper mail in this day and age) telling Nakvoir that xe'd be better off destroying the gene, and themselves. Incredibly, from these dry details xe continued exploring whole new planets of mind-numbing humdrum.

Xe began talking about the science behind the gene, and I did my best not to squirm. There was a saying in my company that those who can't understand are the best to sell. We'd be slightly above the level of knowledge our customers possessed, and therefore able to answer questions with confidence. In completely unrelated news, I had been the top seller for the past five years running.

The conversation continued to fields beyond me, forcing me to resort to digging my nails into my thighs in a failing effort to stay awake. What ultimately kept me from tumbling deeper into dream land were these words:

"I'm carrying it inside me right now."

"You're carrying it inside of you, right now," I echoed, certain that my sense of hearing must have malfunctioned. "That is... cautiously experimental at best."

Perhaps it was my imagination, but I felt that Niffle's light next to me dimmed a little then, as if the fuzzy glow bug was scared.

"It is for the best though, since no one would think to look inside me for the Blank Gene." Xe tapped xyr chest. "Think of it as my contribution to science, that I trust in this that much. I don't understand your surprise.

I thought of all the pamphlets GeneCo gave us, tales of science gone wrong when a multitude of species went under the genetic surgery scalpel. Medicine had gotten better from times of hacksaws and hacks (I still remembered reading about lobotomies), snake oil salesmen and the suckers they preyed upon. Was this blind company loyalty? Or did xe trust in everything that much?

"I've been telling you for the past hour that I need to supply it to Geneki for the gene to be improved." Xyr tone was bathed in disappointment, as if I were a child and had forgotten something important. "I need to be at Port Station Muipra for a handover.

"Ah, which is when you'll use that biometric safe of yours."

"No." Xe grinned and tapped the side of xyr head. "A bit of confusion for anyone wishing to waylay me during my journey."

I frowned at the word, recalling the elaborate map at Port Station Creaon. "I didn't think Muipra was on this line?"

"It's not." The end of xyr tail tapped xyr nose. "I am taking the cautious, lesser used route of Crakid to Ater Arms, and from there will continue until I reach my end. Port Station Muipra. And you said you shall be going to Ginerva's?"

"Yes, I'll take the rail and then be met by electric-cart." I nodded, glad that the conversation morphed into something less... worrisome. "If there is any message you wish delivered to either her or your kin, I'd be happy to bring it."

Sure, xe could call, text, or message; sometimes surprises were more fun.

"Please convey my misfortune to most likely be missing the activities. However, if it's at all possible for me to escape work, I shall be there on the final night of Remembrance Day."

I noted that, even though I wasn't sure when that would be; xyr kin would.

"Anything more?"

Nakvoir of Red Light chuckled. "Please tell Ginerva I promise to set no fires, if she promises to set me no passive tasks."

My head tilted to the side. "She asked you to do something and you started a blaze?"

"Please, nothing like that. Ginerva had been using the room as a storage facility for non functional robots, and I took it as a passive-aggressive ask for me to try fixing them. As I mentioned before, I'm a geneticist, not an engineer or programmer, so my brief foray caused a robot to mix up sweeping the floor with cleaning, adding to the idea that fire would purify and sterilize everything it touched."

"That sounds eventful," I said, quite sure my lips were quirking upwards at the edges.

Before xe could add anything, there was a small chime and flash of light in the carriage.

"At Port Station Crakid already," xe said, nodding to me. At the same time there came a knock at the door, which opened to reveal the blue-hued ticket checker from before.

"Arriving at Port Station Crakid for all disembarking," they said, to which I replied with a quiet nod of acknowledgement.

Nakvoir of Red Light was, at this time, gathering all the items xe'd brought with xem. Putting the blanket back into a self-sealing vacuum packet, collecting xyr communications device, and finally snatching the portable safe and clutching it to xyr chest. Then xe stood in preparation.

"Many thanks, Ms. Rolife, for your society," he said, with an old-fashioned courtesy. "I wish you a good-evening."

"Good-evening," I replied, putting out my hand.

But he either did not see it or did not choose to see it, and slightly lifting his hat, stepped out onto the platform. Having done this, he moved slowly away and mingled with the departing crowd.

Curious to see where xe was heading, I leaned forward to stare, and as I did so, the middle of my foot came down heavy upon something and the resulting sound was one of horror at breakage; certainly not a what should issue from a carpeted floor. I scooped the item up, and sighed in relief when I realized it was Nakvoir's—unbroken—tablet, set to display a book titled Light's Survival Through Space. With everything to grab, and in general being anxious about testing something, this must have fallen from xyr inner pocket. The tablet was metalic, like most electronics, but thankfully had been protected with a plastic case, which, I saw, my accidental step had caused to half-come off at the moment. I forced it back into the shape it belonged in, then sprang for the front door now empty of passengers leaving the spaceship.

The blue-hued guard was there, checking the tickets of all disembarking, but I shook my head as they turned to me.

"If there's spare time, I need to return this to my travel companion—xe just got off and I'm sure xe hasn't left the port station yet."

True, I was meeting xyr kin later on, but even if the book xe'd been reading, Light's Survival Through Space didn't catch my interest, I was enough of a reader that I wouldn't deprive anyone of their material. Waiting for the next bit of information was horrible enough without having it literally being held in another location altogether.

"Less than five minutes. Be quick, because there's no delaying the schedule if you're late."

"Understood." I smiled at them in gratitude, then raced from the gate to hopefully catch a glimpse of Nakvoir. Running as quickly as my body and the beings milling around would let me, I made my way about the large port station, and only saw xem near the end of my time.

But I did see xem, moving against a flow of beings of all shapes, sizes, and saturations. One who walked past me reminded me of a hedgehog with the number of quills their body produced, though walking on two legs. Doing my best not to be distracted, I drew closer, observing that xe was meeting someone who hadn't merited an introduction during our hours of boorish details. They talked as they walked, gaining distance on me, but I thanked the stars of coincidence as they slowed down and moved to the side to continue their conversation.

I made straight for them, taking in the signs and neon colors so I didn't lose them. And it was a very brightly clear area. Each being was well lit and I could distinctly see both of them. Nakvoir of Red Light and the probable human xe was talking to. They had enough gray to their skin that there was possibly Martian in their family. Regardless, the color went with their red hair, brushed beard and mustache, and he wore a brown jacket with pants the color of beach sand. I couldn't think of how old they were since there were, at last check, well over a hundred youthening agents on the market.

Pounding hard on the ground, I continued making my way, calculating in my head that I could just get to xem, hand the tablet over, and make the spaceship by pure nanoseconds. I must admit, the people around me were not as happy as I was. I may have kicked, elbowed, and jumped my way to Nakvoir and xyr friend, only to be knocked down by a family with a small hill of suitcases. As I got to my feet, there was a whistle and a shout directing me back to the ship.

A check—they were no longer there.

"What?" I muttered. I stared at the area as if doing so would bring them back, but of course, the only thing that happened was a last-minute announcement stating that anyone boarding the spaceship needed to be doing so now. "They were right there!"

The passengers going wherever sidled around me and raced away before I could shout any more.

"Where could they have gone?"

"Don't know what you're talkin' 'bout. Saw you." The person next to me stood up and dusted off their pants. "Didn't see no one else."

A whistle shrilled throughout the station, and when I turned I saw that the guard, near the door, was waving to get my attention.

"That's your ship?" There was an ugly laugh. "You're gonna have to run for it."

They were right. I barely made it before the forcefield came down, and for all my good intentions, I still had the tablet, annoyed passengers, and from the look the guard was currently giving me, they weren't pleased either. But, gaining my breath back bit by bit, I settled down in my carriage and tried to think about something else. Anything else.

Yet my brain continued to loop what I had seen. There they were, and then they hadn't been. No nearby door, window, or staircase to go through and disappear. Nowhere to go, and clearly they had. It was not worth thinking about, not when I had work papers to go through, or could even pursue the tablet left in my care (though I'm sure there was a password to wander anywhere besides the currently open book). Suffice to say, the rest of the time I had on the ship, that was what preoccupied my mind. All the way from my station port to the monorail, from the monorail to the ecology-cart, and from there to Mrs. Ginerva's estate.

The distance was eaten up quickly, two hundred and ten kilometers in less than an hour, but as usual when a person is trying to be at an occasion on time, there were little slips through which minutes disappeared. I ended up arriving right as the first course was being served, which gave me the confidence to arrive even later. Directing the program to drop me off at the guest house first, I stole more time to appear less disheveled from travel.

"Welcome to Harmonious Melody Estate, Ms.Rolfie Ann," I heard as the door scanned my eyes.

"And a good evening to you, Mrs. Ginerva," I said. While she was my friend, she'd often complained about not being taken seriously unless people used her title. Her build was slight, since her family had a subset of the Manelae species in their nearest branches, and if a person thought she was completely human, then they assumed genetics weren't in her favor. With the exception of her crow's feet, she looked as if she was fifteen years old. I told her again and again that I could help her seem older, or at least not fully human, and time and time again she waved my offers of genetic manipulation away.

Personally, if it was me, I would have had fun with the options available on the market. I already did so, actually, by giving myself eye and hair colors other humans didn't have, and a tail that I could use as another hand. That bit paid for itself years ago with how many people had ordered their own tail after seeing mine.

"If you hurry," my host said through the comms unit, "you'll be able to meet a few of our friends before the main course is served. The Nasbils, and Captain Ronesse will be staying over for the night as well, but the others are only here for the food."

"And company," I called out as the door dilated open and I could enter my given room. As often as I didn't come here, it still felt like home. Welcoming me back was a cheerful yellow wallpaper with brown 3D lattices holding up several different flowering species. I took a few seconds to inhale the perfumed air.

"I'll give you five minutes. Use the sonic scrubber, re-do your hair, and put on something a little more colorful than a black sweatshirt with black pants. We'll meet in the drawing room."

"Your wish is my command," I responded, heading straight into the bathroom for a quick sonic shower. I did my best to hurry myself along, but it seemed as if everything I could fumble, my body decided to do so twice. Therefore, even though I'd been given a slice of time, I arrived much later than anticipated, filing in to sit in the only empty seat, which was next to a couple I didn't recognize.

While I remember everything now, there are times when I wish I didn't. And I won't go into detail. Let me simply swear that I would have rather talked with Nakvoir once again than sit through the petty problems and grievances that beings who think they are better than others vent in the presence of their "peers." As the Avicon say, "Usoer pieczna, trywp aaltas," which can be loosely translated to Standard Galactic English as "The truth is loud when liars feel safe."

My chair was about halfway down the table, so I was within earshot of all. When the conversation couldn't get any more prideful or snobbish (which made me wonder why my best friend bothered to invite these beings at all), I gave into an impulse to change the topic.

Kopard of Unseen Light was carving up the second part of the feast, bird carcasses drenched in sugar and spices, and the plates used for the soup and salad starter had just been whisked away. With everyone else silent, and my serendipitous placement at the table, it would be easy to regal everyone without having to repeat a word.

"I wanted to say, Mrs. Ginvera, I found myself keeping company with a friend of yours earlier today."

She perked up at that, and I could see her thinking who would be out this way without already being at the dinner table.

"Really?" asked Kopard. Xe sliced into the first breaded bird on the table, carving it in equal parts for all the guests. "Who?"

"Well, they said that they would try to come for your Christmas and day of remembrance celebration if possible."

"My brain is drawing a blank on names," Kopard admitted, exchanging a look with her. "Mrs. Ginvera?"

"It could be Zagui. Ze's due to be in the area for a crafting market." She looked at me, then shook her head. "And I think that's incorrect."

"I'll give you a small hint. Xe's a near relative."

Instead of helping clear the confusion, I watched as it grew worse.

"We've no family coming near any time soon," Mrs. Ginerva said, passing around the small plates she'd filled. "So I'm not sure who you thought you met."

"No one else besides Nakvoir of Red Light! Can you believe that?"

Kopard of Unseen Light laid down xyr carving knife and fork, then let out a grunt. Mrs. Ginerva whistled something back in acknowledgement and he went into the nearby kitchen.

"And xe said that this time, xe promises not to cause a fire if you likewise promise not to give xem broken robots to fix."

I looked about me, realizing slightly before I finished that I was the object of unsettling stares. It was as if I had said something wrong, or stumbled across a cultural line no one had thought to warn me about in the beginning. Wishing the words unspoken, but still not knowing why, I closed my mouth and bit my tongue, not daring to mouth the beginning of another phrase. For at least five minutes there was damning silence around the table, and then, thankfully, Captain Ronesse threw me a lifesaver.

"You have been away for a while, if I recall correctly, Ms. Rolfie Ann? For how long, if you care to refresh my memory?"

"About three years, give or take a few days," I answered, secure in the knowledge that those words shouldn't shock anyone. "I sell genetic insurance to people who are requested to undergo alterations."

There were other words I kept hidden inside, such as a generous thank you to the older being for redirecting the conversation's flow. His small questions were easy enough to answer, and I worried I gave too short replies to truly get a conversation started, but he knew the audience at the manor better than I, and so whatever uncrossable bridge I'd stepped on was not mentioned again. Even so, there lingered in the air invisible chains that refused to let laughter ring true. What had been a dull conversation was now downright tedious, and I wasn't sure which was worse for my friend.

A few who finished dinner (and were fit to burst) staggered out into the living room to continue talking about things there—and possibly watch something from Mrs. Ginerva's collection of rare Earth movies—while the rest remained to put spoons to pudding. I took the opportunity to re-sit myself next to the good captain.

"What did I say that smelled like a wet dog?" I asked in a whisper.

"Nakvoir of Red Light," came his reply. "You mentioned xyr name."

Now I was even more confused. "I saw xem only two hours before on the spaceship; what of that was enough to murder the night's atmosphere?"

"An astonishing thing in and of itself," answered the captain cryptically. "But first, I have to ask again. Was it honestly xem that you saw?"

"As sure as I would have been with my mother or sister," I answered, growing a tetch annoyed at this continued miscalculation of my integrity. "Why is this so surprising?"

"Why?"

His tone dropped to the undertones of a whisper until I was leaning close enough to scent the pudding's chocolate on his breath.

"Because Nakoir of Red Light fled three months ago with the Blank Gene, and no one has heard from xem since."

Nakvoir of Red Light had fled three months back, and yet I had seen xem only a few hours ago! As for why xe'd done that, Geneki had come calling the next day, asking where their Blank Gene had gone. The being had not only been carrying it to their research facility, as xe'd told me, but had been a research subject xemself by having it inserted within xyr person! Was ever a story so strange? If xe'd taken it, how did xe dare show xyr face again? And if xe hadn't taken it, what had xe been doing during this three-month vacation?

Asking these questions provided no answers—even if everyone at the table was think-ing about them. There was no easy solution of course, and I found that the longer I dwelled on the combined facts, the more I doubted any reply I'd be able to make. Captain Ronesse had nothing more to offer either. Mrs. Ginvera, who took the first opportunity to explain the situation, was more astonished at the information I'd delivered, and she came to my room that very night; seeking a conclusion neither of us could arrive at.

"I will not ask you if you could have mistaken Nakvoir—I know that's impossible; the action, if not the being."

"Thank you," I said, nodding to her. "I might not have held a firm friendship with xem, but you're right, it would be impossible for me to mistake xem for a stranger."

"It's not only that. Xe mentioned that we've been trying to add another to our family, and xe would be the only one, outside of us, to have that information." She paused. "How did xe seem to you?"

"Somewhat older, though I had thought that simply the years when I saw xem. Con-siderably more anxious, with worry lines galore."

"Enough has happened to force that look upon xem," she said, sighing. "No matter if xe's innocent or guilty."

"In my own thoughts, I believe xe is innocent." I thought back to the being I'd met in the carriage. "Xe talked openly and at great length about what xe was doing. There were no signs of increased anxiety when the guard popped into our carriage, and there was neither shame nor embarrassment on him."

"That in and of itself is strange, though," she said, running a hand across her face. "Xe is normally quieter about the work xe does, and not one to talk about it... Did xe actually tell you xe was testing out the Blank Gene?"

I nodded.

"Well... Kopard of Unseen Light has an idea about the whole situation. Xe may be right."

I motioned for her to explain, and so she did.

"Xyr thought is this. In the beginning, xe was tempted to sell off the Blank Gene, and xem stored it inside xem as proof, for the highest bidder, that it would work. Then, once the first part of the plan had finished, xe had second thoughts and went into hiding from everyone. At this point, it's been long enough for xem to realize what a horrible idea xe'd had, and you saw xem when xe was returning to the Blank Gene to the company.

That's why xe fancies xe's come back. To beg forgiveness from the company and continue working for them."

A laugh escaped me before I could stop it. "I think that last bit might be impossible. A business is not going to care about a person's feelings, their excuses, their 'I did a bad thing, I'm sorry, please take me back.' That's for beings to feel about others. Corporations care about credits. That type of forgiveness is unknown."

"Honestly, I fear the same..." she trailed off and shrugged. "And yet, there is no other conclusion I can come up with for this scenario. Tomorrow, we can go to Port Station Tilara and question around. By the way, Captain Ronesse mentioned that you picked up Nakvoir's tablet."

"Here." I took it and handed it over.

Mrs. Ginevra took the tablet and flipped it over to its back for an examination. "This is without a doubt Nakvoir's tablet. I've seen xem use it often. And if you look here, this bit of filigree, it's actually a monogram with xyr initials and house name. If there was ever a time when xe had a paper book, xe would emboss this upon the first few pages."

"This at least offers proof that I wasn't dreaming."

Mrs. Ginvera sighed. "True. And I wish to continue speaking about this with you, but dawn comes early and I'm keeping both of us from our dreams."

She stood up, placed the tablet down on the nearest counter, waited under the doorway for the lights to settle, and then went back to her room and loving partners. "Goodnight, friend. And thank you for the hope you've brought. We'll talk more in the morning, and remember that I am more than willing to go with you and help in whatever fashion might be needed."

"Thank you," I yawned, stretching. "I might put that promise to the test tomorrow, but for now, rest is calling. Goodnight."

That was it for the night, and the next time we met again it was in the breakfast room. I gave in and relished the hearty meal before me; handmade sausages, flipped eggs, buttered toast. In contrast, Mrs. Ginevra waved off her normal buttermilk pancakes brekkie and subsisted only on a glass of lemon water; it was clear she hadn't slept well, even if I had, and that essence perfumed the air, pushing me to eat as quickly as I dared so we could get to the bottom of this mystery.

Within the half hour breakfast both guests and family had finished, and after seeing the Captain off, Mrs. Ginerva and I were on our way to the nearest port.

"It might be better for us to go a little further and arrive at Port Station Tilara instead of Port Station Microv. We're at a position equal between the two of them, so usually the decision is Microv since it's smaller and less crowded. Going there more often, however, means they'll be more likely to bring up nasty rumors and salacious details, ignoring any truthful information we're looking to find. All the officials there know that Nakvoir of Red Light as kin, and, well..."

She let her words wander and I nodded. The discussion would be painful if brought up to people who could use this against the family in other matters, such as zoning, voting, or simply community snobbing.

I agreed with her so she reached forward, changed the directions of the electronic cart. We were on the smooth road to Port Station Tilara to see what truth we could scare out of beings.

First, we decided to ask the port-master our questions. Better to ask a person who was bound to remain in front of us if the others in the port were elsewhere engaged in business.

He was a very tall fellow, with a thick scarlet tail and pink spike starting from a crest at the top of his head. Straight to answering, he said that yes, of course he knew Nakvoir of Red Light. The being was commonly seen around Tilara. In fact, xe is known because xe was so easy to pick out.

"I'd see zem here at least four or five times a week, at least three months ago. Our famous crumble cakes and spicy foods lured xem here, I'm sure." His comb pulsed from small to large and back to small with air at his excitement. "Would you like to know where to get my favorite crumble cake?"

We shook our heads, but it didn't matter as he gave away his secrets even as we tried to let him keep them.

"Nakvoir of Red Light hasn't been back since, but I've heard the rumors as to why..." He rubbed his comb and paused. Mrs. Ginerva made a noise of protest, but I put an arm on her, told her there was no need for us to make a fuss which would attract attention, and she quieted down.

"Yes, we've also heard the rumors," she said, strengthening her tone, "and we know that Nakvoir stands accused of stealing the Blank Gene. The reason we are here at the moment is to ask if anyone has seen or heard from xem lately."

The answer was quick. "No."

I must have made a face since he was quick to add that it was possible, but not probable, that another person had information they hadn't yet shared.

"Xe would have used Tilara sometime yesterday."

The port master shook his head and his crest wobbled. "Honestly, I feel Tilara would be the last place xe'd show xemself. We have several branch offices of Geneki built here, and with the reward they've posted asking for information about their product, along with a picture, there wouldn't be a being around here who wouldn't know Nakvoir by sight, and at any glimpse of xem, be reaching for theri comms units. And this information's been available since xe disappeared last 35th of Inze."

"A reminder, Rolfie Ann, that our months have thirty-sex days each," my friend muttered, putting a hand on my shoulder. In a louder voice, she addressed the port master. "And yet, she claims to have sat with Nakvoir in her carriage yesterday all the way from Port Station Creaon, and that xe stepped off at this very port."

"Impossible!" replied the port master, crest wobbling again with how forcefully he'd stated that.

"Why?" I asked. "Just a bit earlier you said possible, if not probable."

"Again, no other port on this entire planet would be as familiar with xem as this one, and if xe was trying to abscond with that unique of an item—not to mention stay away from bounty hunters, then being here would be like a captain piloting their ship straight into a sun; futile and painful. Someone would have collected the credits."

I nodded. What he said were only facts even as what I knew to be true countered them. "Can you tell me who was working yesterday? Who might have seen us?"

"I think I already know the answer, but there's no harm in allowing you to know, I guess." He opened up a tablet and sorted through the data. "Exactly as I remembered. Aesse Amin."

"Can you direct me as to where I can find him?"

The port master laughed, took me by the shoulders, and spun me around. "See that berth right there? Number three? He'll be coming through with the express going to Port Station Exclite, and his spaceship will linger here for several minutes."

"Wonderful," I said, nodding. "Come along Mrs. Ginevera, let's take up positions at either end so we don't miss him."

"Or," said the port master, "I can let him know there are two lovely beings looking to talk with him, and he'll make his way here while he can."

I smiled. "That works just as well, thank you."

The three of us waited in that area, with only the port master working. I'm not sure where Mrs. Ginevra's mind wandered, but mine went to recognizing that this was a set of strange circumstances I'd found myself in. That's where I stayed, wool-gathering for a bit, until one of the newer spaceships grew much larger in size.

"This would be the express," muttered the port master, checking details on multiple tablets now, since the port had gotten busier.

We waited, and less than twenty minutes later, the ship docked, the passengers had alighted, and I recognized the blue-hued being lopping down the plank.

"If you have a few minutes to spare, these ladies had something they wanted to ask you about Nakvoir of Red Light," the port master said, introducing us and our reason within the same breath.

The guard looked at me first, then at my companion, then at me again.

"You I recognize, but I don't understand your connection to Nakvoir."

"Xe's my partner's kin," said Mrs. Ginevra.

"Ah. Then I'm sorry to hear about the problems ze has brought upon your house." As he said that, both of his hands were raised palms up, quickly flipped over, and then smoothed the invisible air beneath them.

The gesture may have brought him comfort, or was a reaction similar as when humans said "bless you" after sneezing. Either way, he waited until both hands were down before speaking, and I made a mental note to research later on what the translation of the gesture meant.

"Nakvoir of Red Light... What about xem?"

"Would you recognize xem if you saw xem?" asked the port master before we could say anything.

"Even before the bounty went up, I would," he answered confidently. "Why?

"Was he on the 4:15 GS express from Port Station Creaon yesterday?"

"Xe was not."

I held back the urge to groan and instead interrupted to ask him how he could answer so positively.

"Because as part of my duties, I'm to observe each carriage to make sure the number of beings in the carriage is the same as the number of beings who had a ticket. Smaller alien species will sometimes trick larger ones into buying a single fare, but they falsely call themselves pets so as to pocket the fee." His tone turned sharper. "I would take an oath that Nakvoir of Red Light wasn't there, even though you were. I remember you. New to me, since I haven't seen you before in life, but I do recollect your photo. You were the only one in the carriage, and you nearly missed going to the next port."

"True," I said, rubbing my chin. "But there was another person in my carriage."

"My understanding was that you were traveling alone," said Aesse Amins.

"Not at all," I said, some heat coloring my voice. "I had a fellow-traveler with me the entire time, and who alighted at this port. In fact, xe was the reason I almost missed my ship as I was trying to give xem the tablet they'd forgotten."

"I do remember you mentioning that, yes," said the guard, "but if you'd had a companion, I would have seen them on the screens."

He snickered at my open mouth.

"It is a big spaceship, ma'am, and in this day and age there are cameras. I don't have to walk up and down the spaceship, poking my head into every carriage to make sure things are going well."

A flicker of rage ran through me at the thought of being watched without my knowledge. The port master must have known why, since he put a hand on my shoulder.

"The cameras do not look straight into the carriage. They keep watch on the entry and the number of people who should be in the carriage. If more than that number exists, we know someone was skipping their fare." He shrugged. "If less of that number exists, then we know we have a murder."

Something on one of his tablets began screaming in digital anguish, and with a muttered patch he excused himself from our group.

"You were standing by the ticket scanning machine just before we entered the station," I stated.

He nodded. "That would be correct. Tickets need to be checked before people leave."

"You must have seen xem since he was getting off then."

"You were the only one in that carriage, and the only one I saw leaving from it."

I exchanged glances with Mrs. Ginerva. Had the guard been bribed?

"If xe had been aboard, I would have seen xyr ticket like all others, and yet I still say in all confidence that I didn't." Aesse Amins checked the time. "I need to begin getting ready for the next launch in five minutes."

"One last question," asked Mrs. Ginerva, desperation tinging her words. "Is there any possibility that you could have failed to simply see Nakvoir?"

"No."

"Are you certain you did not see xem?"

"As stated, I would take any oath stating that I did not see xem. And I dislike to imply that this lady is telling falsehood, but I would be willing to also take an oath that this woman was alone the entire way. If there's any further questions, I assume the security cameras can help you. It's time for me to do my job."

And with that the blue-hued guard gave a polite wave, turned around, and repositioned himself at the ticket gate for the spaceship. We could only stand by as the engine started again and the spaceship, after collecting its passengers, flew on to the next port.

The two of us waited, looked at each other, and finally, I spoke first (a rarity when Mrs. Ginerva was involved, to be sure).

"Mr. Aesse Amin has chosen to keep quiet on some aspects, I'm sure of it."

"Do you really think so? Why?"

"If he could see me plain as sunlight at the door, then he must have simply ignored Nakvoir's presence."

"Well... there is one thing that is not impossible," Mrs. Ginenera said, holding my hand and squeezing it. "And please, think no ill of me when I say this, but maybe you simply fell asleep and dreamed everything?"

I looked at her in frank confusion. "Could I have heard the details about the Blank Gene that are not accessible by the public? Can a being dream up a thousand and twelve boring details for a job they have never been taught? Could I have known that he was carrying the Blank Gene in his body?"

"You work at GeneCo, I'm sure you must have insider access."

"What about being told that story about the broken robots?"

The only other person who could have told me about that was Mrs. Ginevra, or Kopard of Unseen Light, and neither of them had.

"Finally, what about the tablet? It's made of plastic and other electronics, not dream-stuff."

She put up her hands and shook her head at that. "You're right, you're right. Where else would it have come from? These whole twisting facts and circumstances will need a better detective than myself to piece the truth together."

"For the moment, then," I said, taking her arm. "We might as well go and enjoy a good meal. Home, or out?"

And that was how our journey to Port Station Tilara ended, with the area's well-known desserts settling in our stomachs.

I had not been with my friend for any longer than a week before I received a summon requesting my presence at Geneki. My attendance would be a favor and they would be in my debt if I could meet them at a special board meeting not too many days in the near future. There was nothing further mentioned, but my understanding of why this company, at this time, was requesting me was clear. They knew about my unofficial questions at Tilara, and now they had official queries for me.

Still being hosted by Mrs. Ginerva, she was kind enough to take the time to back up to Port Station Creon with me, stating that if all went well she'd love to take me out to celebrate. I'm pretty sure that if what we were doing didn't swing in an optimistic direction, then she would be just as happy to give me a little treat or two to get over the shock.

We took an earlier spaceship—one not from the express line that Nakvoir had taken—and amid the noonday hustle and bustle for lunch we found ourselves at a looming gray building, having been directed there by a tiny flying robot flashing my name.

Once inside, and taken to the eleventh floor, we found ourselves under the direct gaze of precisely thirteen collected beings.

"Ms. Rolfie Ann..."

"It's fine," I murmured to Mrs. Ginerva. Sometimes I forget that, for all the lovers she'd taken, she hadn't had much exposure to the true collective of non-humans in the galaxy. In my case, it's like the annual conferences I attend on behalf of GeneCo. There, I encounter every imaginable combination of DNA—horns, scales, feathers, glowing skin, fire, and so much more. If I tried to mention all the differences between known species in the universe, I would run out of years before finishing the list.

The room itself was half-lit, half-dim, most likely a compromise between the night walkers and day walkers. The coloring was mainly white, black, and gray between the walls, floor, and ceiling, giving the place an oppressive feeling even though I assumed the original wished for result was an evenness and openness which had, sadly, escaped.

I, once I announced myself, was kindly received by the leader, who asked Mrs. Ginerva to sit quietly behind me and fetched me a seat to take after my questioning was done. The discussion began at once when the door hummed shut. As thought, recent statements of mine concerning Nakvoir of Red Light had come to their attention, and the entire assembled group wished to hear my account.

First, I was asked mainly about the character in question. Did I know Nakvoir well? Could I pick xem out of a crowd, identify xem on sight? When was the last time I'd seen xem?

All of the above I answered in the affirmative, until the last question.

"O.E. standard December 4th of this year was the last time I saw him. I'm sorry, but I don't know the day in the calendar you use," I added, apologizing.

There was an explosion of movement and noises from those seated around me, and the same request was asked via several trans-communicators; where and how had I seen xem.

My reply was the honest truth. I met xem in a first-class carriage of a spaceship running the 4:15 express from Port Station Creon to Port Station Exclite. Xe entered my carriage just as the ship took off, and xe'd gotten off at Port Station Crakid while I'd stay on until Port Station Tilara.

The next question was harder to answer quickly. One of the members asked if I had any communication with xem during our travels together. Without going into each and every boring detail we discussed, I spun some of the information together and condensed what had been hours of talking into a single thread. Nakvoir's deluge of details about the Blank Gene and a bit of Geneki as a company.

They all listened to me with rapt attention, and as I talked I noticed at least one of the beings taking notes. When I finished with my words, I produced something a bit more concrete, the tablet xe'd dropped. I had been worried that no one would recognize it. That Nakvoir picked it up recently specifically for the journey. But as the leader took it and opened it to the same page I'd seen in Light's Survival Through Space. As it passed from hand to tentacle to paw to claw to limbs which didn't have descriptive human words, the tablet's design was recognized by all, and it was evidence of my words.

When the leader asked if there was anything else I could add, I shook my head and took a seat in the chair previously provided to me. Thankfully, there was a glass of water as well since all this explanation had given me a parched throat. As I downed a quick glass, the note taker touched a silver communications nodule, summoning forth the guard I remembered from that day.

Aesse Amin had his story to tell, and he was examined as thoroughly as I had been minutes earlier. Sipping water simultaneously kept my mouth closed, my incredulous snorts to a minimum, and was able to keep both my hands occupied. He, too, knew Nakvoir of Red Light well enough that there would be no mistaking xem for anyone else.

He remembered his day on the 4:15 GS express we'd both taken, and he remembered me being in a carriage all to myself.

That was where our narratives completely differed.

He was utterly positive that I had remained alone in my carriage all the way from Port Station Creaon to Port Station Tilara. As I was ready to take an oath that my statements were true, so was he. For him it was that Nakvoir of Red Light had never been on the spaceship in any way, shape, or fashion. My carriage would have registered as having one being inside it when he'd checked my ticket at Port Station Tilrara, and the records showed that it had been at zero.

"This should be easily double checked by security, correct?" asked one of the council beings.

Aesse Amin shook his head. Focusing on his suddenly low voice, I heard that the observation tapes for that time period had been ruined by a technological glitch.

"If you had seen Nakvoir of Red Light, what would you have done?"

"I would have quickly and quietly overridden the private door lock with emergency code number two to keep Nakvoir locked inside, then contacted the council at once.

With the two of us giving clear, confident, and assertive tales, I noticed several of the gathered beings were showing signs of puzzlement.

"You hear the same words that we do, Ms. Rolfie Ann," the leader said to me. "Two truths running away from each in opposite directions. Do you have anything to say for yourself?"

I spread my hand wide. "I can only repeat the truth of what happened as I saw with my own eyes; the same, I assume, that Aesse is doing."

"In essence, what you are saying is that Nakvoir of Red Light disembarked at Port Station Crakid, and that xe knew the private keycode to be a part of your carriage."

"Xe was not the first to exit when we pulled into Crakid, and neither was he the last to alight, which means xyr ticket should have been checked. The spaceship had settled in nicely, and it was after that when xe left our carriage. While I did not watch to see which door xe exited through, I did notice that xe was met by a friend."

"An acquaintance? Were they close enough for you to cast your eyes on their features?"

"Yes, and I did."

"What do you remember?"

"All of it." I gently touched my right temple with two fingers. "My job requires me to retain a vast amount of knowledge, and so I have memory enhancers, which are also to my advantage during times like these. As for the being they met, my words can hopefully paint a picture. The other person was slightly taller than I am, possibly human though there was evidence of Martian in the gray cast to their skin, broad shouldered, red hair, with a neatly trimmed mustache and beard, and he wore a brown jacket over a pair of sandy pants. As for his age, well... in this time period, he could be anywhere between twenty and a hundred."

"Do you remember seeing Nakvoir of Light leave Port Station Crakid with this person?"

I hesitated, then shook my head. "Yes, and no. I saw them meet, begin to talk, and then nothing. Losing sight of them might have coincided with them leaving the port, but I only know enough to guess, and with my spaceship ready to leave without me, my mind turned to other, more important matters."

The leader and Mx. An-tu (for that was the name I heard the note taker called) discussed together in tones quiet enough that the rest of us in the room were leaning toward them in the hopes of hearing anything. One by one they whispered out to the being on their other side, and as this continued, several looked suspiciously at the guard. I could see that so far, thankfully, they were still on my side. My evidence remained irrefutable, and we might have had similar minds in expecting to see Aesse Amin and Nakvoir of Red Light collaborating.

"On the day in question, for how long did you ride and guard the 4:15 express?" the leader asked.

"The entire way down and back again," he replied, a confused look ripple across his face. "From Creon to Exclite."

"Why did you not finish your shift at Tilara? Express ship guards aren't supposed to be traveling the whole way."

One of the other members cleared their throat: "That used to be the rule, sir, until it changed the year before last. Express train guards are to be on their train the entire way through, setting aside illness or emergency."

The leader nodded. "In that case, we would need to refer to the ports' day books, and the ons they'd give regular ships, to check who was working when."

Mx. An-tu frowned, then nodded. "Our timetable is in a non-changeable format, and the most up to date one would be with any of our pilots. Thankfully, however, we have one currently in attendance and will be able to prevail upon him."

A quick telecommunications call, and everyone in the room was waiting in various stages of patience.

The captain came. He looked like a fellow human, slightly taller than shorter, he had a red beard gracing his face, just under his nose and above his upper lip, spreading out to trace the outline of his chin. Between his bottom lip and chin, there was a lighter patch of gray.

His eyes were covered with a visor, but when he entered the room it switched to translucent, so I could tell his eyes were green. Tall, or at least taller than me, he was lean, flaming at the top of his head, and with a strangely anxious manner of walking.

"Captain Baltao, thank you for bringing the monthly port work schedule. We shall endeavor not to bother you for anything further."

"Happy to oblige," he said, handing over a tablet. "And you're welcome to keep this as I need to be off. I've made a copy for myself, so I'll collect it when I return."

"Thank you," said the leader.

I was so surprised at seeing the man from the port, here, in the flesh, that I didn't speak when he was in the room, and couldn't move until the door had closed. No sooner than it had hummed shut, though, than I leapt to my feet and flung out an accusatory finger.

"Him!" I declared, all attention on me as my eyes tried to bore a hole through the wall. "He was the same being who met with Nakvoir of Red Light at Port Station Crakid!"

Surprise, shock, and scoffing disbelief echoed around the chamber.

"Be careful, Ms. Rolife Ann," I was warned. "Your words are set to tarnish the reputation of a great captain."

"Well then. The man who just came into this chamber was at the station, chatting with Nakvoir! I am willing for this new information to be a part of my previous oath to tell the complete truth of what I've seen."

With that, everyone turned to Aesse Amin, who shivered under the attention of so many, but continued to stand straight.

"Did you see Captain Baltao Wilkes there, at any time of the day, on, at, or near the port?"

The port guard shook their head. "I did not see him, nor hear of him and his ship that day at port."

Next was a shared glance at Mx. An-tu. "Captain Balto is employed by your section. What can you tell us about that day?

"I do not think he was still in the office on that date, but my days have been busy, and since we do not employ him one hundred percent of the time, it is possible that he took on extra duties for pay, which is well within his contractual rights."

It was at this precise moment that the captain returned with the port logs, the tablet he was holding the one registered and connected to his ship.

"The date in question, captain, is the 4th of Phigaill, and we would like to see what Aesse's duties were on that day."

"I'm not quite sure why you're asking me. I'm a spaceship captain, not a port command unit."

"And yet every captain that has the port as a registration point also has access to the work logs." The leader waved at everyone seated. "None of us are able to do that, so it's luck and fortune smiling upon us today with your presence."

"Why," whispered Mrs. Ginerva next to me, "would the captains need, or want, to see who was working when at the port?"

"In case they have any questions about inspections, who was sufficiently bribed enough to allow items to be stolen, who is in charge of making sure the port's payment has been paid. Port guards have about a thousand and one jobs in one location, let alone if they follow captains along for the journey as protection."

It didn't take long to find that indeed, Aesse Amin had been on duty that day, checking the communal spaceships before they headed for their next port. A truth I had known all along since I'd seen that visage on the 4:15 GS express from Port Station Creaon to Tilara.

I watched as the leader leaned forward, checking with a few others before abruptly, and in a tone honed to a razor-sharp edge, looking the captain in the face and demanding to know where he'd been on the same afternoon.

"Me, sir?"

"Is there another Captain Baltao in this office? The afternoon and evening of the 4th of Phigaill? That is what we'd like to know."

"I was here, actually, picking up packages to be delivered." He shrugged. "And if I'm not currently in residence, then I'm out among the stars somewhere and my ship's log can prove that."

Even though the words sounded good, I would have sworn before another board that there was trepidation in his tone. The look of surprise upon his face, I concluded after a careful, lingering look, was natural enough.

"There is a possibility that you were absent on that afternoon, in the vicinity of Port Station Crakid?"

Captain Baltao shook his head. "Not at all. I haven't had a moment's peace or rest since early spring, as Mx. An-tu will be able to confirm."

The being politely placed two of their hands on the right side of their body. It was a gesture I'd learned at work. With both hands on the same side, they were indicating a confidence of the truth, while at the same time being "unbalanced," and signifying a slight margin of error.

"Indeed," they added, "I was busy enough during that time period, a body slipping in and out would have been easy to miss. However, they had a solution to that. With a wave of her tail, she typed out a message and asked the rest of us to politely wait.

One minute turned to five, then ten, and finally, a shorter version of herself walked into the room. The only difference between the two was fur, height, and the new person wore a thick red visor.

Their testimony corroborated what Mx. An-tu had said, clearing the captain.

The leader cleared their throat, and I caught a brief flicker of them rolling their eyes; a purposeful human action making their annoyance neither hidden nor unseen, since they weren't human.

"Did you hear that, Ms. Rolife Ann?"

"Yes, I did."

"Did you have any trouble understanding the words?"

I took a deep breath through my nostrils; "I heard, and yes, understood, but my knowledge remains rooted in truth.

"And yet, I believe some of us here, listening to you throwing out times, people, and places which don't match, could venture onto a different reason as to why you believe all of this. Simply put, you dreamt too deeply, and when finally woken you mistook them for real happenings. I think none of us here can say that we haven't done the same at some point, but none of us went on to further accuse other beings with only the information provided in our mental wanderings." The leader motioned to Captain Baltao. "A dangerous habit of the mind to allow development in, and one which might lead to damaging results when trotted out into society. As a captain, his reputation needs to be impeccable, and your baseless accusation might have put him in a perilous place with family, friends, and his job—if it weren't for another impeccable reputation confirming an alibi."

I opened my mouth to reply, but was cut off and given no time to defend myself.

"It is my opinion, members of the board, that we have given this matter enough time and attention. Ms. Rolife Ann's evidence was disproven first by Aesse Amin's, and then with Captain Baltao Wilkes's information her second part was disproven. I would venture that there is more than enough evidence to conclude that Mrs. Rolife Ann dreamt a reality which was vivid, and needs no more time being jawed about."

If there is anything more annoying than to find positive deeds and words met with disdain, dismissiveness, and disbelief, I do not know what it is. This attack upon my evidence, upon my character even, made me feel impatient. It was not only from the leader, but others in the room, and each jab of insolence wounded me further. Mx. An-tu's coloring along the lines of her face was proof that they were bored. Worst of all was the little smug half-smile sitting on Aesse Amin's face, right above where their fangs jutted out from.

Then I looked to the captain, and discovered that his reaction was the worst of all; it was a mix of emotions, vitriolic spiteful smirking with more than a hint of jubilation and celebration. For a few moments, his look made me question myself, my sanity, and my own being. Who was I to come here and claim that I'd see him? Why was I attempting to create an ill wind between him and his employers? Absent with or without leave, who was I to judge? In fact, hadn't I in my youth skived off from work with no repercussions?

All of this nibbled at me and irked me a lot more than I should have let it. As I asked—begged—for the board to remain attentive to what I had to say, Mrs. Ginerva pinched and pulled at my clothing impatiently.

"It might be best to let everything drop," she whispered. "Allow Nakvoir of Red Light xyr sullied reputation. The leader's correct in that this sounds too much like a dream for them to ever take it seriously, and the more you say, the more your own reputation is damaged.

The thought that I would allow personal gain to preside over the truth... I almost snapped at her then and there, but there was something everyone was still overlooking, and I was determined to speak on it. It was a possibility that I had been dreaming. However, it was truth that I had something tangible, which could be smelled, touched, tasted, seen, and felt, and it was yet another truth that it couldn't have possibly come from any mere dream. With a slight bite to my own words, I asked the beings gathered around me if the tablet was part of a shared dream.

"Indeed, that is the strongest point of evidence in your favor," the leader replied. "Your only point, as all others have been negated by witnesses. A tablet is only an item, however, and I would like to put forth that this one might not actually belong to Nakvoir of Red Light. May I see it again and study the embossing?"

"A tablet is a tablet is a tablet," I agreed, handing it over to him. "However, there are none others that bear this embossing, except for the ones in xyr personal library."

He examined it, mouthing something I could neither read nor hear, and then passed it to Mx. An-tu, who took it with their prehensile tail, turning it over and over again as they examined it. Finally, they shook their head.

"It is from xyr personal library, and that embossing is something I remember perfectly, every curve and edge; when I'd first happened upon it the design had intrigued, and I'd begged xem to let me copy it for study; I have seen it, and traced it, more than a thousand times since. This is Nakvoir of Red Light's tablet for certain. And, though I am in agreement with whose tablet it is, how did it come into the possession of Ms. Rolife Ann?"

"I've already said how and can only repeat my words," was my biting reply. "I found it on the floor of the carriage after Nakvoir of Red Light had disembarked. I attempted to run it to xem before the spaceship continued on, and that was when I saw xem speaking to Captain Baltao Wilkes, both hunkered down in conversation." Once again, Mrs. Ginvera caught my hand, her nails digging deeply into my skin.

"Look at Captain Baltao!" she whispered, nodding her curls in the direction of the man. I turned to where the captain had been previously standing, and saw him making his way towards the door on wobbly legs, shivering as if we were outside playing in snow, and yet there was an unnatural flush about his face as well.

Suspicion welled within me, and before I could think to nay-say what I knew was correct in my bones, I rose from my seat, snatched his wrist as if he were a child intent on running into traffic. With a flourish spun him towards the beings in the room. This work of mere seconds was something that caught no attention, and yet my cry did.

"Is this the body, the presence, the attitude of someone who truly knows nothing?"

A quick check around the room—finding frowns, flared noses, and even hearing a slight hissing—told me that my suspicions were agreed upon.

"Captain Baltao Wilkes," came the command. "If you know anything about this situation; the being involved, the item, or even about the timing, you had better speak now."

Unable to slip out of my grasp (with all the times I'd traveled, I'd created a healthy workout habit to stave off boredom), the captain shook his head and continually denied his involvement.

"Unhand me!" Again, he tried to get me to let go, and yet again, he failed.

"The question is: did you or did you not meet with Navoir of Red Light at Port Station Crakid? The answer is either true or false, and if true, you will have many more questions to answer in the near future."

Captain Baltao gurgled in a similar manner a fish might, when caught by crab claws.

"I was gone! Planets away. There is nothing more to answer, nothing to confess, as I am innocent!"

"Planets away... The precise location being...?"

"I had four weeks' of allocated time off and I used it—Mx. An-tu—they know I had the time, that I earned it fairly, and I was using it as intended in Tholmu. All that time I was in Tholmu!"

I looked around the room as whispers abounded, notes were written, and, I assume, translations were sent. Seeing that the good captain was acting... Well, not himself, I noticed that someone must have either sent a message or hit an alarm button because shadows soon appeared to guard the door.

"What has you and your ship being in Tholmu have to do with anything?" asked the leader. "Why are you just now mentioning Tholmu? We were talking about the stations on Zilia 3FI, our planet."

"I believe he is referring to the time he was taking leave, in the middle of Inze," said the secretary. "A little before Nakvoir of Red Light disappeared."

"I didn't even know of this person, hadn't even heard of xem until the rumors started."

"Easily said, if not proven," commented the leader. "In the meantime, since the need to call for higher authorities has yet to appear and I am a local judge in duty as well. If you offer no resistance, and confess, those actions might serve you better than to keep denying any involvement. As for the person helping you—"

Captain Baltao let out a howl that, in my opinion, would have fit a dog better than a human. At the end of it, as if the action had taken all of his spirit, he fell to the ground.

"No one helped me. Not friend nor family nor acquaintances. I was alone, and my confession is this, I didn't mean to harm xem! I was only interested in obtaining the Blank Genre to help lever myself out of debt. Do you know why humans make for poor space captains? Our bodies cannot adjust to the radiation bouncing through the blackness, and

I spotted a way to bypass that. I swear, I didn't mean to harm, only hinder; have mercy on me and let me go!"

"What horrible puzzle are you playing with your words? Spit it out; what do all of those words put together mean!?"

"What does it mean?" repeated Mrs. Ginerva next to me, her usual kind voice laced with pain and hurt. "It means, as sure as we are on Zilia 5F1, that murder had been committed."

"No!" screamed Captain Baltao, looking up from where he was floundering on his knees, and somehow he was just now finding the strength to defend his doings. "Not murder! I didn't mean to kill xem—I only wanted to steal from xem! All alone I continued to make bad decisions, yes, but I never planned for murder!"

The room was silent, except for his screams and I assume the translators in beings' ears which were calmly and cheerily making the screams understood.

"Horrible excuse for a being," interjected the leader after a few silent moments. "There is nothing more I can do with your confession than call for justice."

"You led me on," Captain Baltao shouted back. "You urged me to throw myself upon the mercy of this room!"

"And none of us here were expecting such a betrayal of your beliefs, your community, your very soul! This room can offer nothing more but words of anguish and horror! As well as summon those who can do more to your corporal body. My only advice is that, when they do come, you submit, admit to everything you've done, and commit yourself to whatever punishment they give you. When did this happen?"

The guilty captain managed to get to his feet, though he leaned heavily on a nearby wall. The reluctant answer sounded far off, as if he was plucking it from the aether and cradling it gently in his hands to give.

"On the 33rd of Inze. Galactic Standard date 53829."

It took a second for my neurons to translate that to the O.E. I was used to; July 22nd.

Which any being who could count knew came before my trip. I looked at my old friend, and Mrs. Ginerva looked at me. Upon my face, I'm sure, was a strange sense of wonder. On hers, I suddenly saw the color shift from a flirty rogue to a pallid white.

"In this age of science and facts," she whispered, eyes growing wide. "Who was that on the ship with you?"

Who, or what, had I seen in the spaceship? We, myself with the help of Mrs. Ginevra and her partner, have come up with a possible reply. I know in my bones that I talked with Nakvoir of Red Light, the true being, at the same time xyr body had already been given as a gift to Death. I also know that it used the mannerisms of that being, it gave me information that I could not have learned from any other being, and I was guided by a past vision made of light as to who the other person involved in this murder was. Our reply is a mixture of knowledge gained from the last passage read in the book (provided with a bookmark), a better understanding of how death occurs in Lodiers, and mixed with the little bits of excitement I'd been given by my Blank Gene-enthused coworker. Let me try to lay out our idea in a single sentence: the unconscious mind took the last idea it had read about, used the Blank Gene that Nakvoir had given to test on the way over, and created a being of light that had survived long enough to meet up with me. The only thing we weren't sure about was how many memories could be contained by such a body, and how long it could truly survive as Nakvoir of Red Light.

How Light Survives in Space, the open book that I'd found in the tablet upon the first leg of my travels, was in fact Nakvoir's which xe was reading (no doubt in my mind about it), and upon further inspection, my old-fashioned carriage was the same one that poor Nakvoir had last used as well. It had been taken out of circulation for inspection (clearly not cleaning) as the tablet had doubtless been dropped, unnoticed as xe'd disembarked and been found by Captain Baltao. I'd been the next person to use the carriage for travels, and by that very coincidence, the person to find it.

I dislike dwelling upon the sordid details of the murder. If a being desires more of them, then all they need to do is watch the video confession of Captain Baltao Wilkes, free for all to see via a download on the galaxy star network. There's enough to be said that the spaceship captain, wishing for more money without any health downsides, was in the loop to know when, where, and how Geneki was going to use the Blank Gene for (misguided in his opinion) diplomacy. With this he made the determination to ambush Nakvoir of Red Light along the way, use the Blank Gene for himself, and be on his way to a more lucrative career.

What happened, straightly, is thus. He took paid holiday from work to give himself a legitimate excuse in the eyes of his employers; for his family, he told them that he was needed to captain a rare flight to a secret location. He went to Port Station Crakid for a friendly ambush of Nakvoir of Red Light. They met on the platform, Captain Baltao mentioned that he was there to supply the private flight to finish the rest of the journey, and supplied enough details, knowledge, and confidence that Nakvoir of Red Light was taken in. Then, when they were strapped in for take off in the private spacecraft, where both were sitting up front, the co-pilot seat belt lock was overridden, keeping the unwitting Lodiers trapped. After that it was a matter of dribbling a drugged beverage down xyr throat, waiting for it to take effect, and when it did, jettisoning the corpse so that it would be pulled into an uninhabited planet's atmosphere and burnt upon arrival. He hadn't taken into consideration how a non-human body would react to a human amount of drugs. Which was why Nakvoir of Red Light's body had been able to use the last few unconscious minutes to change to xyr DNA; allowing xem to be a creature of pure light and shadow; memories living just long enough to take a chance on my showing up to cobble together a slight reenactment before disappearing for good.

Interestingly, once having murdered Nakvoir of Red Light, he realized there was no way to actually use or sell what he had taken and he'd never opened the biometric lockbox to realize the Blank Gene had never been in there. Since it was such a unique item—the only one of its kind in existence, to my knowledge—selling, leasing, renting, or involving another person and having them know about the Blank Gene would allow them to go to the authorities—or continue the item's deadly inheritance. He also had to forfeit using it as it was intended since he wasn't going to be able to explain how he'd gotten, legally, any of its effects. So Captain Baltao went back to work, didn't use the Blank Gene as he'd originally wished to make his body immune to the ravages of deep space travel, and believed himself luckily clever that everyone around him thought Nakvoir of Red Light had vanished with the Blank Gene.

Murder was still murder, however, even if a small part of the being was still alive months later. Captain Baltao was given over to the Red Light clan, and the last I heard about it, he was to be a caretaker for the next several hatchings. Considering that humans don't live long enough for Lodiers to give birth twice, let alone several times, his DNA was changed so that he would live (without illness or accidents) for the proper amount of years to carry out his sentence. He can be found on the planet Hamath, deep inside Lodier's territory, if there is anyone wishing to find him; as far as I know, there has been no one looking for him.

The Four-Fifteen Express was originally written by Amelia B. Edwards and published in 1867. The original story would be classified as being in the Gaslight fantasy genre, with a setting from the 19th or early 20th century, usually (though not always) set in England and focuses on supernatural elements. When I was invited to join an anthology put together of retold public domain stories, I thought it would be interesting to give The Four-Fifteen Express a sci-fi setting and see if the supernatural could be explained by alien genetics mixed with technology we certainly don't have today. And that's how this novelette, 4:15 Galactic Standard Express, was written. I hope you enjoyed reading it and will check out Amelia B. Edwards' other works (as well as mine).

AUTHOR SIGNATURES

Thank you for picking up the story and sharing in the joy we felt creating these short stories.

Find more of our books and these authors daily on Twitch! WriteTeam!

Tiana LeBeau

Phoenyx Lee

Find more of our books and these authors daily on Twitch! Write Team!